GRAND SLAM

BE A GENIUS!
READ THE SERIES.

Baseball Genius

Double Play

Grand Slam

BASEBALL GENIUS

#3: GRAND SLAM

TIM GREEN · DEREK JETER

JETER CHILDREN'S

ALADDIN

New York London Toronto Sydney New Delhi

ALADDIN
An imprint of Simon & Schuster Children's Publishing Division
1230 Avenue of the Americas, New York, New York 10020
First Aladdin hardcover edition February 2021
Text copyright © 2021 by Tim Green
Jacket illustration copyright © 2021 by Tim Jessell
All rights reserved, including the right of reproduction
in whole or in part in any form.
ALADDIN and related logo are registered trademarks of Simon & Schuster, Inc.
For information about special discounts for bulk purchases, please contact
Simon & Schuster Special Sales at 1-866-506-1949 or business@simonandschuster.com.
The Simon & Schuster Speakers Bureau can bring authors to your live event.
For more information or to book an event contact the Simon & Schuster Speakers
Bureau at 1-866-248-3049 or visit our website at www.simonspeakers.com.
Jacket designed by Heather Palisi
Interior designed by Mike Rosamilia
The text of this book was set in Centennial LT Std.
Manufactured in the United States of America 0121 FFG
2 4 6 8 10 9 7 5 3 1
Library of Congress Cataloging-in-Publication Data
Names: Green, Tim, 1963– author. | Jeter, Derek, 1974– author.
Title: Grand slam / by Derek Jeter and Tim Green.
Description: First Aladdin hardcover edition | New York : Aladdin, 2021.
Series: Baseball genius ; 3 | Audience: Ages 8–12 | Summary: Jalen DeLuca can
analyze and predict almost exactly what a pitcher is going to
pitch, but without the statistics he has on the pro players, Jalen finds
success to be extremely challenging, especially with all the extra drama
of his mom coming back into his life.
Identifiers: LCCN 2020018033 (print) | LCCN 2020018034 (ebook)
ISBN 9781534406711 (hardcover) | ISBN 9781534406735 (ebook)
Subjects: CYAC: Baseball—Fiction. | Mothers and sons—Fiction.
Classification: LCC PZ7.G826357 Gr 2021 (print) | LCC PZ7.G826357 (ebook)
DDC [Fic]—dc23
LC record available at https://lccn.loc.gov/2020018033
LC ebook record available at https://lccn.loc.gov/2020018034

1

JALEN WAS TOO AMPED UP FROM HITTING THE
championship winning home run to leave the field of
Harvard Stadium. He'd never experienced anything so
thrilling. Could anything ever again be as exciting?

Then the answer appeared out of nowhere.

There she was, tall and upright, with skin as dark as
those enormous eyes. She was elegant and majestic, wearing an electric-blue dress with an inky-black flower pat-
tern. Her cheeks had lost some of the roundness he'd seen
in her picture so many thousands of times, but the thinner
face made her cheekbones more pronounced, reminding
Jalen of his best friend Cat's mom.

He knew who she was. She didn't have to say it, even

though she did, and the words were the sweetest sounds he'd ever heard.

"Hello, Jalen. I'm your mother."

Jalen's eyes darted between this amazing woman in the blue dress and the woman with her, Emery, the private detective he'd hired. Stepping forward, Emery nodded. "Meet your mom. Elizabeth."

Ever since he could remember, Jalen had longed for his mother's return. Now, this surprise reunion unleashed a million thoughts and feelings. His mind filled with questions, but his throat choked back any words.

He couldn't stop looking, comparing himself to her. He was almost as tall as she was. Suddenly his mother flung open her arms, reached out, and hugged him. He hugged her back fiercely, wanting to be sure this was real.

"My baby," she said with her nose buried in the dark curly hair near his ear. "I am so sorry."

"Everything's okay," he said, overcome by her closeness and fighting not to lose it.

She squeezed him even tighter.

"Did you see my hit?" He pulled back, but she kept hold of his hand.

"I did see—a home run for the win. It's a good sign." She smiled, and her teeth sparkled in the late afternoon sun. The bright blue dress she wore reminded him of blue paint in the art room.

"Sign?" he asked.

"For us. That it will be good." She glanced at everyone standing around them in silence. "Your friends?"

"Yes." Jalen turned to them, gesturing with his free hand. "JY—James Yager from the Yankees. Maybe you recognize him."

"I'm sorry that I don't, but I'm glad to know you. Please call me Liz." She shook JY's hand. "When Emery found me, she told me you were helping Jalen with his search."

"Glad to," JY said.

"This is Cat, my best friend, and her mom, Mrs. Hewlett, and Daniel, my other best friend."

His friends shook hands and Cat's mom said, "So very nice to meet you. You have a fine boy."

"Fine." His mother sighed and looked at him with just the hint of a smile. "I have a fine boy."

"I think we'll give the two of you some time without us all gawking," Cat's mom said.

Emery patted his back and said, "We'll talk later."

Jalen's mom was still holding his hand, but then he pulled away, uncertain how he felt. Unsure how to act.

"What about the team? The bus?" he asked, feeling

guilty that thoughts about the game and his dad were suddenly crowding his mind.

"They can wait fifteen or twenty extra minutes," JY said. "I'll text Coach Allen. He'll understand. My gosh, who wouldn't . . . it's your mom."

Cat's mom began herding Cat and Daniel and JY and even Emery toward the parking lot.

"I'll get your gear to the bus, amigo." Daniel headed to the dugout.

"Thanks," Jalen called, turning back to his mom.

She reached out again for his hand. Beyond her Jalen could see the rows of seats so recently filled with fans and food and noise and celebration.

"Jalen?"

He knew that she wanted him to look at her, and so he did. "Yes?" Her big dark eyes glowed. A black band held her long curly hair—so like his—off her face.

"At first I didn't let myself think about you. It hurt too much. And then I had a chance to come back to the States and perform. I have a weekend gig in Boston. When Emery first contacted me, I couldn't believe you'd forgive me. . . . I came to the games yesterday, too." Tears spilled down her cheeks. "I'm sorry to get all jumbled up. I'm just so excited."

He could see how badly his mother wanted everything to be better—all at once—but he shook his head. "I don't get it, just not thinking enough about your own son. Not caring enough about me to call or write. Not ever."

She stretched out her other hand and touched Jalen's arm, blinking back tears. "I know. I'm sorry. For everything."

The only response Jalen could muster was to listen to her words and nod, as his eyes searched her face.

"Huh. Well." His mom forced a smile. "Let's get you on that bus."

She turned, and he went with her, still feeling like it was unreal. "Um, what happened? I mean, why did you go?"

"Didn't Fabio tell you?"

"Dad said you had a dream. He said you needed to go."

She relaxed a little. "Yes. That's right. I'm a singer. I had an amazing opportunity. I thought it was worth everything. I believed I could make it big. I still do, but nothing is as easy as you dream it will be. I've been so close, Jalen. . . . I've learned that anything worth having never comes easy."

"I'm gonna play in the big leagues," he said, jamming a thumb into his chest.

"See? That's your dream." She stopped and gestured with her hands. Her long fingers fluttered like wings. "You need to follow that dream. We don't get many chances to make it come true."

A jazzy ringtone shattered the moment. His mom fumbled in her purse, found her phone, and listened intensely.

"Oh no!" she said. "I'll be right there." She ended the call and looked at Jalen.

"Jalen—I've got to run. I'm already late."

Jalen couldn't believe it. "But we just met."

"I'm so sorry, Jalen. I have to go."

She gave him a quick hug and dashed away.

His eyes followed her until she reached the corner of the stadium.

"Mom!" he shouted.

The flash of her bright blue dress was the last image he had before she disappeared from sight. She never looked back.

2

THE WEIGHT OF CONFUSED DISAPPOINTMENT
filled Jalen's belly, sickening him. Just breathing was diffi-
cult. He stumbled toward the team bus, putting one foot in
front of the other. How could she just disappear like that?
Again? It all felt unreal—until he stepped up into the bus.

Cheers erupted from the team. Kids were jostling in the
aisle, slapping him high five and calling him Champ.

"All set, then?" Coach Allen asked Jalen. "Are you all
right?"

"Yes. Thanks, Coach."

"Okay then. Find a seat. We're ready to roll, Fred."
Coach patted the driver's shoulder. "Let's get this team
of winners back to Bronxville." He turned to the rowdy

Bandits and shouted, "Gentlemen, we are the team to be reckoned with!"

Jalen found his seat halfway back, across the aisle from Daniel. The bus was big enough for everyone to have his own row, but Daniel was waving to him and slapping an empty seat, so he slid over as the bus hissed and rumbled away.

Daniel was excited. "So . . . ?"

"What?" Jalen asked.

"Why'd you say it like that?" Daniel scowled.

"Like what, Daniel?"

"You said 'what' like I was dog doo-doo on your shoe. I just want to know about your mom. Emery said she's a star."

Jalen thought about how his mom hadn't even looked back. "Sorry. I'm not up for it now." He was too confused to want to talk about her.

Daniel stopped scowling and kept his voice low. "Okay, amigo. You know I'm here for you."

"How about that game?" Jalen said, anxious to change the subject.

Daniel shrugged. "We won, but Charlie Kimber got pulled from the order so you could bat—his dad saw it and got bent out of shape."

"What? You think Charlie hits a home run if he's batting instead of me?"

"I don't! I'm just telling you."

"I understand, though," Jalen said suddenly.

"You understand?" Daniel was puzzled.

Jalen was thinking about how his mom had left him, probably to sing somewhere, when he said, "Kimber's father cares more about his son than winning a game."

Daniel was quiet, knowing Jalen well enough to sense that he was serious. Then Daniel got serious. "But that's not even why I wanted to talk to you. Amigo, you're not gonna worry about all that after you see this."

Daniel held up his phone. He had a YouTube video cued up. "I think this thing is about to go viral, if it hasn't already. It's got twenty-six thousand views."

The weight in Jalen's stomach sank further as he took the phone, because the first frame of the video was his own face.

3

ONE LOOK AT THE YOUTUBE VIDEO WASN'T ENOUGH.

Jalen had to watch again. He wanted to be sure of what he thought he saw.

He looked up at Daniel. "Who took this?"

Daniel shrugged. "Someone sitting near us."

"Just some . . . random fan?" Jalen let out a gust of doubtful laughter.

"Could be. People video all kinds of stuff. But . . . you think Jeffrey Foxx is behind it?"

Foxx was the Yankees GM who wanted to get rid of JY and who knew that Jalen had been helping the Yankees star boost his batting average by signaling—during JY's at bats—exactly what the next pitch would be. The rest of the sports world knew Jalen and JY had a connection but thought it had to do with Jalen's father, Fabio, and what JY called the "lucky calamari" he ate at the Silver Liner before the Yankees games.

Fabio's Silver Liner Diner had drawn attention not only from a Twitter storm that JY created, but from the regular media as well. The flood of people who wanted to taste the lucky calamari, and a rave review in the *New York Times*, had prompted an investment group to offer funding that would quickly franchise his father's restaurant, creating a chain of Silver Liners in different, as yet-unnamed locations.

It was a dream come true for Jalen's dad, and people were calling Jalen "the Calamari Kid." But his close friends called him a baseball genius.

Foxx was no friend. He knew JY wanted everyone to think he'd gotten out of his late-career batting slump on his own, not by some trick with a kid that no one could explain.

Even Jalen couldn't explain it. It just happened. He'd watch a pitcher for a while, and then he'd just know what the next pitch was going to be. Once he got locked in, Jalen could predict every pitch to come.

"I think Foxx would do anything he thought would hurt JY."

Daniel frowned. "Everyone loves JY."

"Not Foxx! JY made Foxx look bad when he showed

everyone his career is far from finished. And Foxx is one of those people who can never be wrong, even when he is," Jalen said. "Especially when he is."

Jalen looked down at Daniel's phone and saw himself in the video, signaling two thumbs-up—which meant a changeup was coming. The frame swung away from Jalen, then froze, and a circle of light highlighted JY at the plate, staring intently in Jalen's direction before turning his attention to the Red Sox pitcher. The highlight faded out, the pitch came in, and JY knocked it over the Green Monster, scoring what would be the winning run for the Yankees to beat their division rivals.

Jalen saw himself jumping up, screaming, and hugging Cat and her mom before the shot moved to JY rounding the bases. The YouTube title was: "Squid Kid Gives JY More Than Luck?"

"JY is gonna kill us," Daniel said, taking back his phone.

"JY? We didn't post this." Jalen huffed.

"I know, but all he kept saying was that we gotta keep this quiet, and now everyone is gonna know," Daniel said.

The problem was big enough to push his mother's unexpected appearance (and disappearance) to the back of Jalen's mind. He buried his face in his hands and sighed, because he knew what Daniel was saying was true. And he knew it was likely to ruin everything.

4

DANIEL PATTED HIM ON THE BACK. "SORRY, JALEN.
I had to tell you. You had to know."

"I'm not mad at you," Jalen said. "My brain is spinning. That's all."

The bus pulled onto the Mass Turnpike. They rode in silence for a while before Jalen raised his head and laughed at the simple idea that had popped into it. "Daniel, this is easy. I just deny it! The whole thing. It could be a coincidence, right? I mean, we know because *we know*. To anyone else, it's just gonna seem like a coincidence—me giving two thumbs-up and JY going yard—especially if JY and I both deny it. After all, I'm just a fan wishing him luck, right? Thumbs-up!"

"Yeah, but what about the team?" Daniel pointed out. "They all know. Coach Allen knows. He told the guys it was real, and you just signaled to our lineup when Chris was going to throw a fastball, a curve, or a changeup."

"But I know Chris's game." Jalen smiled. He'd gotten special pleasure out of beating Chris Gamble for the championship. Cat called him Jalen's nemesis, but he thought that "nemesis" was too fancy a word for Chris. The coach's son was a bully and his biggest rival. Just the week before, Chris and Jalen and Daniel had been on the same team. Chris's dad coached them, using his position to give his son every advantage over Jalen.

"We just say he had some obvious tells," Jalen said, "and we were kidding about helping JY in a Yankees game. No one is going to think I can really predict the next pitch, especially if I deny it."

"But Coach Allen? He knows," Daniel insisted. "JY told him."

"I think we know Coach Allen is a diehard fan. He won't hurt JY."

"Maybe," said Daniel. Jalen sat back and closed his eyes.

After a time Daniel tapped him on the shoulder. "So, you gonna tell me about your mom, or what?"

Jalen opened his eyes but kept them focused on the back of the seat in front of them. "I don't know. . . ."

He couldn't say the words that kept running through his mind and wouldn't stop: *Why did she come back into my life for five minutes and just run away again?*

"She's so pretty," Daniel offered after a moment of silence. "And . . . she seemed really nice," he added, obviously struggling to find the right thing to say.

"Yeah, well. She is." Jalen didn't want to talk about his mom.

"Yeah. Duh. Right?" Daniel laughed with obvious discomfort, then changed his tune. "Hey, what about the smackdown you gave Chris? Bam! See ya!"

"Anyway, we're celebrating, right? Listen."

There were shouts of the players joking, and laughter up and down the aisle.

"Amigo, we didn't know these guys a week ago, but now we're part of the team," Daniel continued. "We're Bandits!"

"Come on," Daniel said. "Let's go to the back. Gertz and Fanny are doing some kind of finger-puppet show."

"Nah. You go, though." Jalen didn't bother to look, but he moved over to his own side of the aisle so Daniel could get out. He sat down and laid his head against the window before closing his eyes.

Daniel slid across the aisle and put his hand on Jalen's shoulder. "You should come, amigo. You're the big star."

Jalen kept his eyes shut. "Thanks, Daniel, but this thing

with my mom . . . She got some phone call and just . . . disappeared."

"I mean, she's okay, right?" Daniel asked.

"I don't even know."

"Let me know if I can do anything," Daniel said.

Jalen only shook his head. Daniel stood up, paused for a second, then gave Jalen's shoulder a thump before he disappeared into the back of the bus.

When he was alone, Jalen tilted the seat all the way back and closed his eyes again. It wasn't sleep that he was after. Instead, on the movie screen in his mind, Jalen replayed every minute of the time he'd spent with his mom. He saw the sparkle in her dark eyes and studied the smile at the corners of her lips.

It hurt to think he might never see her again. Jalen scolded himself for being negative. She'd come back.

She had to.

5

JALEN HAD NODDED OFF, AND HE WOKE TO FIND
someone shaking him. He looked up at the Bandits star
pitcher, Grady Gertz, offering his winning smile.

"Hey," Jalen said. "Some game!"

Gertzy laughed, closed both hands, and popped them
open. "BOOM!"

Jalen *BOOM*-ed him back.

Gertzy was tall and thin but solid. He waved his hand
breezily through the air. "Bet the other team bus is a lot
quieter."

Jalen laughed.

"That's my man." Gertzy gave Jalen a high five before
he reached into the bulging pockets of his uniform pants

to take out two cans of soda. He cracked them open and shoved one at Jalen. "So, you gonna tell me if it's true that James Yager showed up after the game? Daniel would neither confirm nor deny."

Jalen hesitated. "Yeah. He did."

"Maybe next time you can introduce me and Fanny?" Gertzy wiggled his eyebrows.

"Sure, Gertzy."

"Awesome. Hey, drink up. Here's to champions. Today, and for the rest of the summer."

"Champions!" Jalen clinked his can against Gertzy's and took a sip. "How's Daniel doing with the guys?"

Gertzy snorted. "He's hilarious. That was an awesome catch he made at the end of the game. I think it was good for his confidence. But on to a more important subject: Did you guys actually put a bag of rabbit turds in that Chris Gamble's lunch?"

Jalen burst into a grin. "He told you about that?"

"Ugh! I would've paid money to see it," Gertzy said. "Some serious hot sauce, right?"

"Hot sauce" was Daniel's favorite way of saying, "Wow! Look what just happened," or a substitute for words he probably shouldn't be saying. It sounded funny coming from Gertzy.

"Hot sauce for sure."

Gertzy tapped his can against Jalen's, giving him a smile and a wink. "You should come back to the zone with me and Daniel and Fanny."

"Cool," Jalen replied.

Gertzy headed for the back of the bus. Fanny was the team's redheaded, brick-built catcher. His real name was Justin Fanwell, but he was Fanny to his friends, and they had fun with the name.

Jalen already knew, like everyone, that the last four seats in the bus—next to the bathroom—were Gertzy's "zone." He sat in the far back row with Fanny in front of him. Anyone who wanted to use the bathroom had to pay a toll to Fanny, a toll he claimed was to keep Gertzy from leaving for one of the big national travel teams. It wasn't a serious thing. Sometimes candy or a bag of chips or a dime or a quarter was surrendered. Once, Jalen had heard, Frankie Ortez got by with a bottle cap.

Guys also came back to get in the zone to be part of the action. Gertzy's "guests" got to kneel on a seat or stand in the rows facing him and Fanny. Jalen stopped in the aisle next to where Daniel knelt on the seat, like Damon LaClair and Charlie Kimber across the aisle.

"Jalen," Gertzy said. "Back here and sit your fanny right down."

"Fanny is already sitting down," said the big guy, never

looking up from a ham sandwich he was devouring.

The other guys began chirping all at once.

"You can't argue with a redheaded fanny."

"Hey, keep your eyes off my fanny."

"That's my fanny you're talking about."

"Is that what smells?" Gunner Petty called, walking up the aisle. "I thought it was the toilet, but it must be my fanny."

Everyone laughed.

Gertzy scooted in and made room for Jalen to sit down, patting the seat. Jalen blushed at the special attention.

"Thanks, bruh." Jalen raised the can he was still carrying and took a swig.

Gertzy just looked at him, smiling. "You said that before, my friend. But, now I'm thanking you. You're the one who helped me get on base with that baseball genius stuff. Then you blasted a homer for the win."

"Oh, that genius stuff is just a joke. I can't really predict pitches," Jalen said, loud enough for all to hear. "I mean, I don't have the force." If anyone from the media asked his teammates about the "Squid Kid" YouTube video, he wanted them to think it was a fake.

Gertzy's smile widened. "You can't fool me. I saw you do it. You told me every pitch. Even Coach said it was the real deal."

"It was part luck and part me knowing Chris so well."

Gertzy nodded and waited until Daniel and Fanny began to chat before he lowered his voice. "Okay, I get it. You don't want everyone pestering you, but you'll still help me, right?"

If Jalen made an exception, then he knew he'd worry about things slipping out.

"Oh, come on, Jalen. Baseball is my life."

Jalen knew he should say no.

Jalen wanted to say no.

But instead, he said, "Okay."

6

"HA-HA!" GERTZY CLAPPED JALEN'S SHOULDER
and spoke so no one else could hear. "We are gonna have
some kind of summer, you and me."

"Yeah." Jalen wondered if Gertzy could keep a secret.
He was a really nice guy, Gertzy. On their very first day
with the team, he'd reached out to make Jalen and Daniel
comfortable as the new kids, and because he was the
team's star player, the rest of the guys followed along. "I
hope Charlie is gonna be okay."

Gertzy stopped smiling. "Dude, you gotta stop worrying
about that kind of stuff, right now."

"What do you mean?"

They were interrupted when Fanny's face appeared

over the back of the seat. "Got a customer. I'm looking at a pack of Twizzlers, only a couple of 'em gone."

"That'll work," Gertzy said.

"Knew you'd go for them." Gunner, the team's first baseman, was heading into the bathroom. He was a cheerful kid with wavy brown hair that covered his ears, brown eyes, and an easy, lopsided smile. When he emerged, he said, "Hey, nice game, Gertzy. Nice dinger, Jalen. That pitcher had a bazooka."

"Thanks, Gunner," Gertzy said. "Sweet stretch on that double play in the second."

Fanny, Gertzy, and Gunner bumped knuckles, and Gunner gave them a final nod before loping back to his seat. Fanny tore off two ropes of licorice, popped one in either side of his mouth, and handed the remainder to Gertzy. Gertzy tore it apart and gave half to Jalen.

"This is what I mean." Gertzy held up a wiggly strand of licorice before taking a bite. "Humans like hierarchy. Look at the queen of England, loved by the world. CEOs are paid millions of dollars. No one blinks. Why? People like order, and they like whoever the top dog is to act like the top dog. Not being mean or anything, but just enjoying it without worrying."

Jalen chomped on his licorice like he understood. "I know what you mean."

"Yeah, and even guys like Daniel come around when they realize that's just how things go."

"What's 'guys like Daniel'?" Jalen's stomach tightened.

"Proud. Stubborn." Gertzy shrugged. "Nothing bad, but he's used to being on an even footing with you, and—no offense—he's really not."

"We're all one team," Jalen protested.

"Yeah. That's important, but we all know who's got juice and who doesn't. This is a competitive travel team. Like Coach Allen says, you gotta check your feelings at the door."

Jalen couldn't imagine that Gertzy's words would sit well with Daniel. He peeked up over the seat and was relieved to see Daniel playing some game on his phone, as usual.

"It can change, too, you know. Look at Gunner." Gertzy pointed at the bathroom door. "Two years ago he got cut. Last year he rode the pine. Now he's a core player for us. Get it?"

"Gunner got cut?" Jalen said.

Gertzy nodded. "Then he grew five inches. Then six more, and he lived in the batting cage."

"That's a good point," Jalen said. "Things change."

Gertzy jostled his shoulder. "You got it. Hey, want to run two versus two on *Clash Royale*? You got *Clash*?"

Jalen took his phone from his pocket, beaming, and said, "Let's do it."

Only two weeks ago he and his father had gotten their first-ever iPhones thanks to the recent success of the Silver Liner Diner. The world had opened up for Jalen, not just with games and messaging, but having a phone that actually could go online. He could finally get all the big-league stats at Baseball-Reference and answers to all kinds of questions with a quick Google search.

He powered up and saw he had five voice messages from Cat. He had twelve texts from her as well, and he didn't need to see even the banner line of her texts to know she wanted to talk about his mother. *Not now,* he thought.

Jalen had the *Clash* app loaded, but even though he'd played it often, he hadn't realized there was any particular strategy involved in playing. Gertzy talked him through some moves, and soon they got lost in the world of giants, spiders, wizards, skeletons, and dragons, all battling each other. After about the first half hour Cat texted him again. The banner popped up on his screen with a tiny *ding*.

S'up?

"Not now," he groaned to himself, as if Cat could hear his thoughts. He typed **Clash** and sent the text so he could rejoin the battle. The app was just beginning a fresh game. Their best combination was when Gertzy launched his bomber balloon and Jalen sent his dragon just in front. The dragon absorbed all the enemy fire as it led the balloon across the battlefield to destroy the enemy base.

They were tied in a hard-fought battle with twenty-seven seconds left when Gertzy said, "I got a balloon. You got a dragon?"

"On deck," Jalen said.

Gertzy leaned over and looked at Jalen's screen. "Play your goblin barrel to the right. Then, as soon as you have enough elixir, play the dragon behind my balloon on the left."

The timer already read :19 when Jalen launched his goblin barrel. His finger was poised to strike with his dragon, but he needed more elixir. The seconds were slipping away.

"We got this. We got this," said Gertzy. "Ready?"

"One more second," Jalen said. "And, go!"

In the fraction of the second before he released the dragon, a text banner popped up.

Ding.

???

"Jalen, go!"

"I can't!"

7

JALEN SWIPED DESPERATELY AT THE SCREEN. IT
took three tries to remove the banner and launch his
dragon. The balloon was out front, and it collapsed without the escort. The dragon chugged forward on its own,
uselessly late as the other team destroyed his base.

"Shoot." Gertzy sat back in his seat. "Will you please
stop those texts?"

Jalen hadn't owned his iPhone long enough to know
that was even an option. "Sure. Can you show me how?"

Gertzy disabled the notifications for Jalen's text messages. They got back into their game and played on, winning chest after chest of gold, emeralds, and new cards.
After a while, Jalen's stomach rumbled. Daniel had

disappeared to the front. Fanny made a sandwich run, and they ate while they continued to play.

Before Jalen knew it, it was dark, and they were pulling into the Bronxville Middle School parking lot. The storm that had been threatening all day was aching to break loose as parents waited anxiously under the lights. Jalen let everyone go ahead of him, then ducked quickly into the bathroom. As he was getting off the bus, Fanny put the box of remaining sandwiches on his shoulder, then spilled them all. The rain started while Fanny and Jalen were picking them up.

By the time they finished, and Jalen grabbed his bags from beneath the bus, the parking lot had nearly emptied out.

Jalen was shocked to see Daniel's father's pickup truck at the exit, signaling to take a left on Pondfield Road, headed back to Rockton. He took off running across the blacktop, hoping to cut them off. But when he reached the street, the pickup was fifty feet away.

"Hey!" he shouted, dropping his bags on the road so he could run faster and wave his arms. "Hey!"

The truck kept going. He gave chase as it accelerated, but the red taillights kept getting smaller. He stopped running. When he looked back, the last of the cars were pulling out of the school lot heading right, into the Bronxville suburbs. The bus shut its door with a hiss and began to move, leaving Jalen completely alone.

Jalen dialed Daniel's cell phone, but it went straight to voice mail, which meant Daniel had shut it down. He turned on his notifications, and his phone dinged five or six times. He peeled through them: two from Cat and four from Daniel, asking Jalen if he was going home with him or not. The final text was: **Ok amigo. This makes 4x. If i dont hear back i'll assume ur staying over w Gertzy. I get how u dont want to ride w a guy whos got no juice.**

Jalen raised his chin toward the pelting summer raindrops and hollered with all his might. "Hot sauce!"

8

WHILE JALEN GATHERED HIS BAGS, IT CONTINUED
to rain. He scrambled for the school awning.

He wondered who he could call, biting the inside of
his cheek as he considered his options. His dad was busy
at the restaurant, and he'd be super upset to learn that
Jalen had been abandoned. Call his mom?

"Ow!" Thinking about his mom and that he didn't even
know how to call her had made him bite down too hard.
He rubbed his cheek.

Cat would know what to do. Maybe she could even
help. He felt guilty texting her now, after she'd reached
out so many times and he had ignored her, but he had
no choice.

S'up? Where r u?

He knew she was reading it and waited for her reply. The wind blew rain sideways, under the awning.

"I'm fine," Jalen told himself, wiping his face with the back of his hand before looking at his phone.

Almost home. Stopped for food. What happened w ur mom? Did u see the YouTube video from the game?

Jalen's spirits rose. They'd have farther to drive if they rescued him, but at least they weren't settled in back at home. Rockton was thirty minutes away. He ignored her other questions and typed, **Can u get me in Bronxville?**

She replied, **What happened to Daniel?**

Long story. We got our wires crossed. I'm at school. I'm stranded.

He watched the thought bubble as she read his text. It kept going, and he assumed she was asking her mom. Finally she replied, **On our way.**

Thanks so much!!!

Jalen pulled his bags to the center of the awning. Shielding his phone, he checked out the YouTube video of him helping JY. It now had twenty-eight thousand views, not exactly viral, so that was good news.

He scrolled down through the comments. Good news. People weren't buying it.

Do you seriously think JY needs tips from a kid????

Yeah, JY was a star before the kid was even born.

And, *I wonder how little you've got going on in your life to make a video this stupid.*

He googled "Calamari Kid," but it didn't bring up anything he hadn't seen before. More good news. He breathed a sigh, then wondered how he could google his mom. He didn't even know if she still went by Elizabeth Johnson.

She didn't.

Jalen tried "singers in Boston," but that led him to a bazillion possibilities. He wasn't sure if his mom had a different stage name, either.

Finally Cat texted that they were two minutes away. Jalen stopped his search and stood looking out at the heavy rain.

As the Range Rover pulled up to the curb, he grabbed his gear and ran for the car.

The hatch opened and Jalen dumped his bags before climbing into the backseat. "I am so sorry, Mrs. H. I tried to get Daniel, but his phone was off, and I got hung up on the bus."

"Oh, Jalen, things happen. This is what friends are for." She reached back from the driver's seat and patted his leg before setting off.

Cat spun around in her seat. "I'm the one you ignored."

"Sorry, Cat. I just didn't want to talk about my mom—"

"And I told her that, Jalen." Mrs. H shot a frown at Cat. "It's his own business, Miss Catrina."

"He can talk for himself, Mom."

"Yeah. No, she's right," Jalen told Cat. "I gotta get my head around it."

"Okay. Fine," said Cat, sounding anything but fine. "As long as you tell me you didn't say anything to Daniel on that three-hour bus ride."

"That I promise you."

She studied him. "What happened with you two?"

"He heard Gertzy tell me that there's a few players on the team with juice, and then there's everyone else."

"And let me guess," Cat said. "Daniel isn't a member of the chosen."

Jalen exhaled through his nose. "How'd you guess?"

"Shot in the dark." She went silent.

Jalen broke the silence by handing Cat his phone. The video of JY and all the comments were up on the screen.

Cat's eyes widened. "Whoa," she said.

Jalen nodded. "Yup."

Cat thought for a second. "We'll talk about this later. But right now, we gotta figure out what's going on with Daniel."

9

CAT LOOKED LIKE SHE WAS THINKING AND THEN
came to a decision. "I'm going right down to see him as
soon as we get home."

Daniel's family lived above the enormous stables on
Cat's stepfather's estate. Cat didn't think anything of
hanging out with Daniel and Jalen. She didn't act rich.
She told them more than once that Mount Tipton—the
two-hundred-year-old estate's name—was like a fancy
hotel, not a home.

"You don't need to get in the middle of our mess," Jalen
said.

Cat's mom turned up the radio, and no one spoke until
they reached the center of Rockton.

"The diner or home?" Mrs. Hewlett asked.

Normally, Jalen didn't like Cat's mom to take the gravel drive that wound through the wetlands beside the tracks to where he and his dad lived. Many years ago, when they'd built the new train station, some enterprising handyman had converted part of the old depot into a small dwelling, adding two cramped bedrooms and a leaky shower. One side of the roof now sagged lower than the other side, and the gap had been waterproofed by slapping on a bright blue tarp. "I'll be by this week to fix it," the handyman-landlord kept promising.

The tarp had recently begun to flap in the wind, adding to the run-down look.

But tonight Jalen was too tired to care, and he asked to be taken home. At least it was too dark to see the shabby place when they dropped him off. He thanked Cat and her mom for saving him and waved good-bye.

Inside, he let the door creak closed and the comfort of home wash over him. He left his gear by the door and got ready for bed.

On a shelf in his bedroom, amid the baseball posters and trophies, was an old eight-by-ten framed photo of his mom. It was a photo that had haunted him as long as he could remember. His father once said that she married him to help him get a green card so he didn't have to go back to Italy. He told Jalen she'd gone away to follow a dream.

Now, even though he'd been with her, he didn't know a lot more.

Jalen lay in bed, listening to the rain and the snapping tarp, staring at the picture. Finally he yawned and turned out the light. When his father came in later, Jalen was still awake, but he pretended to be sleeping. His dad tiptoed across the floor and kissed his forehead.

"Jalen?" he whispered, and waited, hovering over Jalen before straightening his back and adding, "Tomorrow, you gonna be so happy. . . ."

Jalen clenched his hands to keep from jumping up to ask why.

10

WHEN JALEN WOKE, A DULL GRAY LIGHT LEAKED
through the curtains. It was already seven, but gloomy.
The rain was still falling softly. Jalen's dad was gone. A
note on the kitchen table said he was going to the market and would be back by seven thirty. There was nothing
about any happy news.

In the kitchen corner, a nest of towels held a large pot.
Steady drops from the ceiling plunked into the pot, which
was about to overflow. Jalen emptied it in the sink and
put it back under the drip. Water now plinked against the
bare metal bottom. He looked at the stream of water running across the ceiling and got angry.

Dressing hastily, he went out, standing back to look up

at the roof. He could see where the tarp had blown back in the night, exposing the bad roofing. No wonder the kitchen ceiling leaked! Jalen had had enough of waiting for the landlord.

He raided his father's tools for a hammer and nails, which he put in a bucket. Then he grabbed a ladder. He started climbing to the lower side of the roof, holding the bucket. His sneakers squeaked and slid on the narrow, wet ladder rungs, and he moved slowly up to the roof. Once there, he breathed a sigh of relief and crawled carefully over to the tarp. He knew his father would have a fit if he knew Jalen was doing this kind of work, but he told himself it had to be done.

Pounding the nails felt good. After a bit, Jalen finished nailing the tarp back on.

Back inside, Jalen took off his wet sneakers and put on dry clothes. The trees dripped with rain, and he wondered if the Yankees would be rained out tomorrow night. They were scheduled to begin a four-game series with the Orioles. He checked his phone for the weather. Rain was forecast to continue through the afternoon before clearing. Tomorrow was fifty-fifty. There were no new text messages. He wasn't surprised about his friends, but he had expected JY to reach out and tell him about the lineup. Was he in it or not against Baltimore?

GRAND SLAM

Jalen had been glad to help JY for free for a few big reasons, not least the glory of assisting one of his heroes and his favorite team. There was the lucky calamari and the way JY had jumped in to get the Silver Liner fixed in record time after the fire. The Yankees star made the connection with Coach Allen that got Jalen on the Bandits. Then last week Cat had negotiated a contract that paid Jalen an incredible five thousand dollars a game!

He shook his head in wonder and thought, *Cat is really something.*

Jalen filled a bowl with Raisin Bran and splashed in milk. He sat at the table, crunching away and wondering if the thing that his father whispered about last night had anything to do with his mom. Did he know she was back? He sure seemed happy.

Jalen couldn't help hoping as he washed his clothes and started organizing his equipment bag. Humming with anticipation of his dad's news, he gave his two bats a polish before stuffing them back inside. He zipped the bag tight just as the rattle of their van on the gravel announced his father's return. Jalen ran to meet him on the front porch.

"Hi, Dad."

His father wore scrubs and a faded jeans jacket. His bald head was shiny with the same rain that speckled his small round glasses. They hugged and kissed each other's cheeks before his father said, "Jalen, is all wet out here— and you with no shoes. Come inside."

Jalen followed, bumping into his dad just inside the door.

"Sit down," his father said. "I make you some break- fast."

"I ate, Dad. I'm good." Jalen stood, eager for the happy news.

His father smiled and chuckled. "Okay, sit down. I got a surprise for you. You gonna be so happy."

"What is it, Dad?"

11

"THE YANKEES, THEY WANT A SILVER LINER RIGHT
there in Yankee Stadium, on the mezzanine. That's your
team!"

Jalen stared at his dad. Finally he said, "What do you
mean? You're going to have a diner in the stadium?"

His father's stout arms—marked with burn scars from
years of working over a stove—were crossed proudly over
his chest. "Yes. A sit-down restaurant inside the Yankee
Stadium! The franchise guys are making a deal today."

"With the Yankees?" Jalen tried to take it all in.

"Yes, because of JY and the lucky calamari! The NYY
Silver Liner Diner will be in Yankee Stadium!"

Suddenly his dad looked at the clock. "I gotta go to

work. I got three cooks coming today. They gonna learn to make *nonna*'s sauce and the calamari stuffing."

"Three cooks?"

Jalen hadn't considered what franchising really meant. He knew they were talking about opening Silver Liner Diners in lots of places right away to capitalize on the Yankees fan base, so of course they'd need other people to cook his father's—or really his *nonna*'s—food.

"You're teaching them to do what you do?"

"Yes," said his father. "Is why they pay me the money."

Back at the restaurant, his father went into the kitchen while Jalen helped Greta, the waitress who'd been at the Silver Liner since the day it opened. Today Greta wore a flowery dress, and her dark, wavy hair was held back with a headband.

"Pretty dress," Jalen said as they set up the tables for lunch. Ever since the diner's popularity had exploded, Greta had upped her game on the wardrobe front.

"Wash those hands, young man." Greta snapped a towel at him, stinging his leg behind the knee.

"Ouch! When did you get so fussy?"

"After I looked up and saw Aaron Judge at table six. What a sweet young man," she called after Jalen as he slipped inside the men's room to escape.

The stall was in use, so Jalen began washing his hands. He was drying them when a man came out of the stall and said, "Hey, Calamari Kid. Nice to meet you."

"Nice to meet you, too. Are you here for the calamari?"

"Sort of." The man turned to the sink but caught Jalen's eye in the mirror as he scrubbed his hands. "I'm point man for the investors, overseeing all the pieces—design concepts for interiors and exteriors, all the advertising, staffing, accounting, and the menu—which is why I'm here today."

"My dad said you're gonna have our diner in Yankee Stadium."

The man shook the water from his hands and grabbed some paper towels, but he wasn't done with his fast-talking. "Yes, a fabulous idea. The Yankees came to us with it last week. They want it to be—for style—'NYY Silver Liner Diner,' which I like. Made me realize this one should be named specially too. Either 'Fabio's Silver Liner Diner' or the 'Original Silver Liner Diner.'" You have a preference?"

"I . . . I don't know," Jalen said. Changes were coming so quickly. "Maybe you should ask my dad."

"Right, I'll make a mental note." The man's excitement actually increased. "This whole thing is a sprint like I've never seen, but I like it, all the elements, the backstory about an immigrant dad and his young son who collide with a sports icon struggling to hang on. Add a pinch of magic, some incredible social media numbers, and a huge shout-out in the *New York Times*, and you've got yourself a winner, right?"

The man winked at Jalen.

"Uh, yeah," Jalen said.

"Well, I'm back at it. Nice to meet you." The man pushed past him.

Jalen's mind was whirling as he finished setting up the tables with Greta. JY had made the Silver Liner Diner famous. What would the Yankees' owner say when he saw the video? Would he still go ahead with the stadium deal?

His phone buzzed in his pocket. He took it out and saw that it was Daniel. He felt light-headed and slightly sick. He held his thumb over the green button, then the red, then green again before he tapped it.

12

"HEY." THE WORD WAS AS FLAT AS JALEN COULD make it.

"Hey," said Daniel.

They were both silent.

Outside the dining room's big picture window, the clouds had begun to thin and the rain had lightened. The sun was trying to break through.

"What's up?" Jalen finally asked.

"So, we got practice today. You believe that?"

"That's how you get better," Jalen said.

"I know," Daniel said, "but we're gone all weekend and next day we got practice?"

"I like practice."

"Yeah, I get it. You're devoted. You're a star. I called to see if you wanted a ride."

Jalen hated the tension between them. "Look, I'm sorry Gertzy said that. I didn't think you heard him. And yes, I want a ride. You know I need one."

Daniel said, "Cat told me what happened on the bus, that you never got my messages. I feel kinda bad about that. My dad kept asking if I was sure you didn't need a ride, and I thought I was."

"So let's go play ball."

Daniel paused before he spoke, "Yeah. Okay. Okay, amigo. Even if I'm just here to make you stars look good."

"You're the real deal. Wait till I see you and tell you what's happening."

"No worries. We'll pick you up at twelve thirty," Daniel said drearily.

As soon as Jalen pocketed his phone, it buzzed. Without looking, he answered.

"I can't say anything now—I have to get back to work."

"Should I call back after your work?"

Jalen's throat knotted up at the sound of a woman's voice. "Mom?"

13

"YES." HIS MOM'S VOICE WAS WARM AND COM-
forting. "I'm sorry if I called at a bad time."

"No, no, no. That's okay. I thought you were Daniel. I can talk." Jalen turned and walked straight into the parking lot with the phone pressed to his ear.

"But what about your work? I don't want to get you in trouble," she said.

"You just . . . disappeared yesterday." Jalen looked around for a rock to kick before he said, "I thought maybe, like, forever."

"Oh no! I was so late, I panicked." She took a deep breath. "I'm so sorry, Jalen. I had an interview with *Downbeat*. That's like *Sports Illustrated* in my world. I just couldn't be late."

"Still following your dream, right?"

"Could we meet somewhere and talk? Did you tell Fabio I'm here?"

"I . . . should I have?"

"Not necessarily."

"He works all the time, and he's doing a really big deal with these money guys. They're franchising the Silver Liner." Jalen realized how fast he was talking. He tried to slow down, but he wanted to let her know how well his father was doing because he'd wanted his parents to get back together for so long. "That's his restaurant that got famous from JY tweeting about the lucky calamari."

"You both must be so excited," she said. "You know, your father came to America to work hard and be a success. He's always been great at the first part. Maybe now he can get the second. His dream is coming true, thanks to you."

Pride bubbled like soda fizz in Jalen's chest. "Well, a lot of people helped, and if his food wasn't amazing, none of it would have happened anyway."

"Absolutely. The man can cook." She paused. "So, can I pick you up somewhere? Is there a good time?"

"Mornings in the summer, I work at the restaurant." Jalen started walking back to the Silver Liner with the phone to his ear. "Where are you?"

"We're headed for White Plains, the Ritz."

"JY took me to lunch there."

"Well, it's close to Bronxville, so . . ."

"I live in Rockton." Jalen stopped on the restaurant's front steps. "But the Rockton team coach wouldn't let me play, and his son's a bully, so when the Bronxville coach recruited me, I switched over right away. That was the Rockton team—my old team—you saw us beat in the championship yesterday."

"It was very exciting," she said, "you showing up at the last minute like that."

"Yeah." Jalen hoped he wasn't bragging. "I'll be at the Bronxville Middle School for practice by one."

"That works. We'll see you then. Can't wait!" she said.

"Wait, 'we'? Who's 'we'?" Jalen asked quickly. It was such a small word, but still, Jalen nearly choked on it as he said it aloud.

But his mom had already hung up.

14

HIS WHOLE COMFORTING IMAGE OF FAMILY
togetherness got flushed in an instant. Jalen stuffed the
phone in the pocket of his sweatpants, then got back to
work.

When he finished a quick lunch, his dad was in the
kitchen stuffing a squid for his audience of chefs. Jalen
gave him a signal that he was leaving.

His dad looked up and grinned. "Everyone, this is my
son, Jalen."

Heads turned. One said, "Hey, Calamari Kid."

Jalen introduced himself and shook all their hands
before turning to his father. "I'm so excited for you, Dad."

His father laughed. "Yes, I know you're excited. Me too."

Fabio turned to the chefs. "My son's gonna play major league baseball someday!"

They had some general comments that Jalen pretended to pay attention to before telling his dad good-bye. The rain had stopped, and the sun shone through the clouds.

Walking home, Jalen buzzed Cat.

Cat knew all about the YouTube video.

"Yeah, well my dad just inked a deal to have a Silver Liner in Yankee Stadium. What if the Yankees owner finds out about the video and pulls out of the deal with my father?"

Cat was quick to see the possibilities. "He could pull out of the deal, I guess. But he could really, really want to go ahead. He's big—he could get YouTube to pull the video."

Jalen pumped his fist. "You nailed it! That could happen."

"If he really cares. After all, publicity is good for business."

Jalen's happiness evaporated when he told Cat about the meeting he was going to have with his mom and whoever was the other part of "we."

"I never thought she'd have someone else. I thought she'd want to be with us—me and my dad."

"You want me with you?" Cat asked. "So you won't be alone?"

Jalen paused. Part of him didn't want to share his mom,

even with Cat. The other part of him worried about going it alone, especially since she was going to bring an extra person.

"Oh, come on," Cat said.

"Sure," Jalen said. "We're going to meet before practice."

"Sweet. I'll get my mom to drop me off."

Jalen was home grabbing his gear when his phone buzzed. This time it was a text from JY.

15

I'M OUT FOR TONIGHT.

In the excitement about his mom, Jalen had forgotten all about JY's game. Now the complication was gone before he even had to face it. He was glad, but he couldn't say that to JY.

Sorry to hear.

JY replied: **Thx. maybe tomorrow. Did u see the YouTube Squid Kid video? Not good.**

Jalen texted back, explaining that he and his friends had no part in the video. He could see that JY was reading it. Then came the reply: **Hey, not a deal breaker. Still, maybe we should take a break for a while. See what I can do on my own.**

A week ago, that text would have shattered Jalen. Now, with his mom back, his father's overnight success, and his own clear path to baseball greatness, Jalen felt like the pressure was off to be JY's baseball genius. He texted back: **kk**.

He gathered his gear and headed for the center of town, where Daniel and his dad pulled up in their big white truck within five minutes of his arrival.

Jalen got in back and Daniel's dad spun around. "Jalen, I am so sorry about last night."

"That's okay, Mr. Bellone. I shouldn't have had my phone on silent" Jalen said.

"Well, next time I won't be listening to this knucklehead son of mine." Mr. Bellone winked and turned his attention to the road.

"What?" Daniel sputtered, but before he could protest, Jalen spoke up.

"If anyone was a knucklehead, it was definitely me." Daniel broke into a smile as Jalen continued, "I should have been with my main man, but I got lost in a video game."

Daniel's dad dropped them at the school parking lot, and Jalen said, "Amigo, I've got to rush through this because my mom is coming. But maybe things will be good. My dad told me the Yankees' owner wants to open a Silver Liner Diner at the stadium! I thought he'd pull out because of the YouTube, but Cat thinks he'll shut down the video."

"Cat's smart," Daniel said. "I bet the owner will keep JY and kill the video." Giving Jalen a fist bump and a "Good luck," he headed off to the locker room, leaving Jalen to meet his mom.

The Range Rover pulled up to the field while Jalen was standing there looking for his mom. He checked the time on his phone as Cat and her mom sat talking back and forth. They seemed to be arguing. Finally Cat got out and her mother pulled away.

"What's up?" Jalen asked.

Cat bumped fists and rolled her eyes. "My mom thought she should also join us. I was like, 'No way.' I'm sick of this 'You're only a kid' garbage."

A text from his mom came in.

Almost there!

"She's almost here!" Jalen shouted.

"Easy, Jalen. You look like you stuck a knife in the toaster."

He looked into her eyes. "You know what I'm afraid of."

"Yes. I know." She took his hand and squeezed as a black Mercedes sedan pulled into the parking lot.

He took a deep breath. "Well, here goes."

Jalen could see his mom through the passenger window, but the driver was hidden by the reflection on the windshield. Jalen's mom waved him toward her, signaling to him as she got out. Jalen glanced back at Cat. He paused and gave her a questioning look.

She shooed him on.

Once she was out of the car, his mother gave him a huge hug while Jalen looked past her. Sitting behind the wheel was Jalen's worst nightmare, live and in the flesh.

16

THE MAN GOT OUT AND CIRCLED THE CAR. HE WAS
tall, at least six foot six, and thin. He wore a light blue suit,
a crinkled dress shirt, and no tie.

"Jalen," said his mom through her smile. "This is George
Compton. George is my biggest fan and my partner."

Did she expect him to be happy? Jalen thought, incredulous. Didn't she know he not only wanted her back in his
life, he wanted her back in his father's life as well? One
happy little family, just the three of them. No one else was
part of it.

Jalen couldn't hide his disappointment. He couldn't
even try.

"A pleasure." George had a smooth British accent and

a silver mane of hair with a prominent streak of black. Weird. He shook Jalen's hand.

The two adults turned to Cat.

"This is Cat." Jalen caught her eye. "She's my best friend."

"And his agent," Cat declared.

Jalen's mom reached out to shake Cat's hand. "Call me Liz, Cat. I like a girl who knows business!"

"So, you're like, my mom's business partner?" Jalen asked George, finally able to squeeze the words past the bad taste in his mouth.

George winked at Jalen's mom. "Well, that and more. Wouldn't you say, darling?"

George had slightly crooked but brilliant white teeth. He kept them largely concealed by lips that looked ready to break out into a whistle.

"Yes, we are also together, outside the business part," Jalen's mom said, patting George's arm.

Jalen glanced at Cat. She gave a slight shrug.

They all stared at one another for a minute.

Turning to his mother, Jalen broke the silence. "So, where do you live?"

"Our home base is London," she said, "but we travel a lot to shows."

Jalen's mom turned her shining eyes to George. "Should

I tell him, George?" Their closeness made Jalen feel sick, and he fought not to turn away.

George and his mom looked at each other for a long moment. Then George said, "Yes, Lizzy, I think you should."

17

JALEN IGNORED GEORGE. HIS EYES WERE LOCKED
on his mom.

"We're thinking about moving to America." She paused, staring at him. "Would you like that?"

"Here?" Jalen asked, his heart thumping.

"We'd like to be able to see you, Jalen. Be as much of a part of your life as you'd like. George can open an office in the city, and I can get to anywhere from JFK."

"Where do you have to go?" Cat asked the question that was on Jalen's tongue.

"Wherever clubs want me to sing," his mom said, "We did Scullers in Boston, and I'm here to be in Tarrytown— at the Jazz Forum!—then, in the future, Philadelphia and DC. At least those gigs are scheduled for now."

Jalen felt like his mind had shut down. He saw George leaning toward him.

"So Jalen, Lizzy tells me you're a baseball player, and a Yankees fan, like me."

"You're a Yankees fan?" Jalen nearly choked on his words.

"Absolutely," said George.

Jalen and Cat glanced at each other.

George went on, "Of course, cricket is my preferred game, but when I spent two years at Columbia University as a grad student, of course I discovered that North America had its own bat-and-ball game. And it had a championship-caliber team a short Underground ride away from campus."

Jalen looked and felt confused.

"Oh, Underground. You mean the subway," Cat said knowledgeably.

"Just so," George agreed, smiling.

Jalen's mom pounced. "You haven't told us what you think about us moving someplace close."

"I . . . that sounds . . . great," Jalen said. He held back and didn't say everything on his mind. He'd loved and longed for his mom his whole life. Even though things were so strange, he felt by the way she looked at him that she loved him, too. Then there was his dad. Fabio DeLuca clearly didn't have the class—or money, judging by the Mercedes—to compete with this guy.

George put his arm around his mom's shoulder and whispered, "Don't rush, Lizzy." He gave her a gentle squeeze. "Slow and steady, right?"

"It's just that I haven't told my dad," Jalen said. "When you disappeared after the game, I didn't know what was going on."

His mom couldn't hold back her impatience. "Should we sit down with Fabio?"

"No!" Jalen was so loud, everyone jumped.

He lowered his chin. "I'm sorry, but I'll tell him. I just have to figure out how."

"I'll tell you how," George said. "Would you like to know?"

Jalen stared into those piercing blue eyes. "Yes."

18

"IF I REMEMBER MY GEOMETRY CORRECTLY," HE said, pointing a finger to the side of his head, "the shortest distance between two points is a straight line."

Jalen stared hard into George's eyes.

"I mean to say," George said in a theatrical hush, "just tell him straight out."

Jalen felt his anger rise, and it felt good. "We're talking about my dad here! I can't just walk into the restaurant and say, 'Guess what, Dad? Mom turned up, and she's got a guy with her.'"

"Of course you can, darling," his mom said. "You should just sit down and tell him straightaway."

"Could we maybe say that you found me?" Jalen asked.

"Yeah." Cat spoke fast when she got excited. "You could say someone retweeted something about him and JY and you saw it when you were in Boston and presto! You came to his game."

Jalen caught her fervor. "Yes, you were doing a show in Boston when you saw it, and you took it as a sign."

Jalen's mom looked at them with obvious disappointment. "When you tell one lie, it makes a crack in the ice. It grows and grows and branches out, getting bigger. You step this way and that way, but any way you go, that lie's already beaten you there, and then you're in it. You're sunk."

"But I don't want to hurt him," Jalen said.

"How much more hurt would he be if you lied and he found out later?" asked his mom.

Cat looked at him with surrender in her eyes.

Jalen didn't like being scolded by the mom who'd gone off to London to follow her dreams and left him behind. He didn't like it at all. And most of all, he didn't like it in front of George.

"Then how would you do it?" Jalen asked.

"Be direct. Sit down with him. Say you reached out to me and I surprised you with a visit. Then tell him I'm moving back, and you'd like to be able to see me." She brushed a long curl behind her ear. "Don't worry. One of the best things about Fabio was that he always had a hard time saying no. He rarely got angry and never stayed angry for long. Isn't that still the way he is?"

"I gotta go practice," Jalen said, suddenly aware of the relief it would provide. He could barely wait for them to be driving away.

Cat was by his side. "Mom went to shop in Bronxville. She's picking me up at three."

They headed for the dugout, breaking into an easy run. All too soon they were on the field.

"Where you been?" Coach Allen grumbled. "This isn't some game we're playing here that you can drop in and out of."

"I'm sorry, Coach. It won't happen again." Jalen meant it too. His MLB dream was still alive, and he wasn't going to ruin his chances.

"I'm sorry too, Coach. I won't let you down on the stats again," Cat said softly. She was going to get the coach to forgive the fact that she'd been at the Yankees game during the championship game in Boston. Jalen wanted to stick around to see her work her magic on Coach Allen, but Gertzy was calling from the pitcher's mound.

"Jalen! I been waiting for you. Let's throw some baseballs!"

"Sure," Jalen said. He stared at Daniel as he jogged toward Gertzy. "I'm just gonna, uh . . ."

"Yeah, go on," Daniel said. "You're not my babysitter."

Daniel wore a grin as he and Jalen bumped fists. Jalen slipped past him, then jogged out onto the field.

While they were doing warm-up stretches, Gertzy whispered, "Bet you a shake I can tell you what the coach says we're doing today—the exact words!"

"No way."

"Hah! Very much way. Coach Allen is like most people over forty. He never hesitates to repeat a good joke or a smart idea. So every Bandits practice starts with the same speech."

Gertzy waved his arms theatrically and cleared his throat.

"Sheesh, you're acting like a character in a kids' film," Jalen said.

"Silence! Please!" Gertzy put his hand on his chest. "'Gentlemen,'" he began in a very accurate imitation of the coach, "'no baseball team ever lost because they were too good at the fundamentals. Therefore, today's practice will concentrate on fielding fundamentals.' From there it varies."

Jalen vaguely remembered the words from the only other practice he and Daniel had been to—right before the tournament. He could practically feel the price of a shake flying out of his pocket. Still, he didn't mind what Coach said if he called them "gentlemen." His old coach didn't even know the word.

As they started with the physical basics—jogging across the outfield with exaggerated knee lifts, shuffling side to side, backpedaling, and more—Jalen felt like part of a unit. Stars and scrubs alike did everything. They were a team learning to get better.

But when they broke into baseball activity warm-ups, the seams of team unity started to fray.

"Okay, genius, let's you and me do long toss," Daniel said.

"We do long toss by position," Gertzy said. "Outfielders together, infielders together, and catchers go off by themselves to practice their magical arts."

After striking a pose of deep thought, Fanny said, "I agree, it really is magical the way I can make food disappear."

Getzy, Fanny, and Jalen couldn't help laughing. Daniel was poised to argue but was waylaid by Coach Miller.

"I'm hearing more excuses than I'm seeing action. Let's get some work in before the end of practice."

"I think Gertzy's right, Daniel. Hey, Gunner," Jalen yelled to the first baseman. "It makes sense for us to toss together, right? Second baseman and first baseman."

Gertzy gave Jalen a secret thumbs-up as all the team members paired off and began tossing at a thirty-foot distance they would gradually expand to over a hundred feet.

That was slick of me, Jalen thought as he stretched his arm out. *Diplomatic, almost.*

19

WHEN WARM-UPS WERE FINISHED, COACH ALLEN
called the team in around home plate. He put his hand on
his chest and said: "Gentlemen, no baseball team ever lost
because they were too good at the fundamentals."

Gertzy caught Jalen's eye and they practically broke
out laughing.

"Therefore, today's practice will concentrate on fielding fundamentals. Catchers will work on the elements of
receiving: framing, blocking pitches, throwing to bases.

"We'll do pitcher fielding practice on the right side of
the infield. Ground balls, short hops, and infield flies on
the left side. Outfielders will work on reads and routes,
catching thrown fly balls.

"Let's get to it, and try not to be sloppy. Practice is designed to make you better players, not casualties."

They did a shout in unison and broke off to their positions. Everyone knew that Coach's warning wasn't a hollow threat. A wildly bad throw could bean a teammate working on a different drill.

Fanny, at catcher, could get as badly dinged by a pitch in the dirt at practice as in a game. And PFP, or pitcher fielding practice, could look like ballet one minute and slapstick comedy the next. There was no denying that getting those game actions right could be the difference between a win and a humiliating loss.

Jalen, Gunner, and Gertz worked at PFP. On bunts that got past the pitcher and slow ground balls that got the first baseman out of position, the pitcher had to outrun the batter to first and field a throw while moving at high speed. The first or second baseman had to lead with his throw to a moving target. The toss had to be fast enough to beat the batter to the bag, but not so fast that it was impossible to catch. After a couple of clumsy efforts, Gertzy and Jalen got a feel for each other's movements and timing. They developed a rhythm, and it actually looked like ballet.

Eventually Coach Allen said that they'd done enough fielding for the day. "It's time for some offense."

"No problem, Coach," Fanny yelled. "My parents say I offend everybody."

"Coach, I think that man is too unhinged to have a bat in his hands," Gunner joked.

"Sometimes I have the same thought," the coach said, playing along. "Still, it's the way we operate."

Coach Miller reeled off groups of names: some to hit in the batting cage, some to shag balls hit to the outfield, the rest to get five swings at live pitching and rotate out. By turn, everyone would do the same work. The coach had put Jalen, Gertzy, and Gunner in the same group with a couple of less accomplished hitters.

Coach Miller stood on the pitcher's mound behind a life-size L-shaped screen, for protection.

"After you," Gertzy said, and made a flourish with his arm.

"Oh, no, after you," Gunner responded.

"No, after you," Gertzy replied.

"Jalen, get in the batter's box and let them work it out," Coach Miller said. "Today we're going to hit to the big part of the field. Everybody hits balls gap-to-gap. Use the big part of the field."

Jalen cringed. He wasn't used to thinking of line drives. He wanted to say, *I mash dingers, not singles. I want to crush grand slams, not hustle doubles.*

The coach's first toss, a typically medium-speed fastball, was irresistible. Jalen hit a rope over the third-base bag. Not what the drill called for.

"Way to make the coaches love you," Gunner called, loud enough to disturb the customers back at the Silver Liner.

Jalen ignored the taunt and dug an unnecessarily deep hole for his back foot.

He thwacked the next pitch foul, getting far out in front.

"Think middle of the field," yelled the coach, "right back at me."

But it only got worse after that. Jalen reached his boiling point quickly. Try as he might, he couldn't get near the middle of the field. He couldn't even keep a ball fair. If he didn't know better, he would have thought he was trying to hit them into the dugout near third base. He wondered what the coach was thinking, what his teammates were thinking.

"Okay, Jalen. Rotate out." It was Coach Allen.

Jalen hadn't even realized that the head coach had been watching. His mind raced, and he saw himself asking—begging—to get back on Chris Gamble's team. He sullenly walked away from home plate and stood silently behind the protective screen when a hand landed on his shoulder.

"Drop the bat and take a walk with me," Coach Allen said.

Jalen's mind flooded with fear as he thought, *Oh, no, it's really happening. He's kicking me off the team for . . . for pulling the ball?*

When they got farther from the field the coach said quietly, "Jalen, I don't know how much coaching you had before you joined the Bandits, but trust me, you're going to have a lot more here."

"Really, Coach?" Jalen felt relieved. "That's what you wanted to say?"

"Oh, that's just the opener. It's a long game. . . . The thing is, you have great athletic ability, no doubt. And you have great bat-to-ball skills. What you have to work on is technique. Technique developed through endless repetition is the only thing that will get you through the failure you're always going to have."

"But—"

"No buts, Jalen. Listen. The best players in the pro game make outs seventy percent of the time. But if you have a .300 batting average, you're a star. If you got thirty percent on a math test, you'd be pretty humbled, right?"

Jalen just nodded yes. It was true.

"You can't hit the ball up the middle at will, and I don't think that's caused by hardheadedness or anything but lack of technique. If you want to play here, you're going to learn how to keep your hands inside the ball. You need to start your load earlier. Get your weight back and then drive forward with your front shoulder in. Keep your hands for last. . . . Do you see?" Coach asked as he executed the motion he described.

"I think I do, but it's a lot to take in," Jalen admitted honestly.

"Hmm. You know, one of the best examples I could give is James Yager. You've seen him play a million times. You could do worse than imitate his approach. You've seen him load his weight, fire the lower half of his body, and bring his hands through last."

"Well . . . honestly . . . I don't really watch JY when he's playing. I don't really watch the technique of any hitter. I'm always watching the opposing pitcher, trying to predict his pitches," Jalen explained.

Coach Allen laughed heartily. "That is what you do, isn't it. Well, not here. Here you work on your game. Agreed?"

"Absolutely. Here I work on my game."

"Let's shake on it!"

20

OF COURSE, WHEN PRACTICE WOUND DOWN,
Fanny and Gertzy and Daniel razzed him about being the
"teacher's pet" and "trying to be buddy-buddy" with the
coach and a dozen other half-joking/half-jealous taunts.

Jalen stayed in control. Coach was making an extra
effort because he thought Jalen was worth teaching. And
that made Jalen feel like his game was going to soar. He
was going to make it.

All he was willing to say to his friends was "hot sauce."
And it drove them wild.

21

BEFORE THEY HIT THE LOCKER ROOMS, GERTZY
pulled him aside and lowered his voice. "You heard of Lakeland?"

"Heard of them? Sure," Jalen bluffed.

"Yeah, only the biggest sports academy in the country. Top players from all over go to school and train for baseball, year-round. They start in sixth grade. Imagine that? And their tournaments are almost impossible to get into."

"Yeah? So?" Jalen swatted at a bee with his glove.

Gertzy rested an arm on each of Jalen's shoulders so he could look Jalen in the eyes. "So, we are in. No one else knows."

Gertzy looked around before continuing. "College

scouts come to this tournament. We're talking SEC, ACC, like Florida State, LSU, Vanderbilt, places that really crank out the pros."

"Yeah, I've heard," Jalen said, desperately wanting to be alone to google on his phone.

"Jalen!" Coach Allen called from behind home plate.

Gertzy glanced nervously at the coach. "Shh. Don't say I said anything."

"I won't. Don't worry," Jalen muttered, then took off like a rabbit until he pulled up short in front of home plate. "Coach?"

"You never used one of these to help you hit, have you?" Coach Allen took up a long stick leaning against the backstop. It was a bat handle attached to a stick that ran straight through the middle of a baseball.

"No." Jalen had seen them and always thought they were a gimmick, a fancy piece of equipment he didn't have the money for anyway. He was grateful Coach hadn't called him over to grill him about his conversation with Gertzy.

"I thought not." Coach Allen took up a batter's stance. "Here's what you do. You begin your swing and stop your hands here, like the handle is a flashlight you're shining straight at the pitch. See?"

"Yes."

"And the ball is down by the handle, but when I finish the swing . . ." He swung and the ball hit the far end of the stick with a loud *pock!* before he handed it to Jalen. "It makes that sound, like hitting a pitch. Try it."

Jalen took the stick and swung, but the only sound was "Umph!" from his gigantic effort. The ball hadn't moved more than three or four inches.

"You're trying too hard. That's what I thought. It's more about timing than strength. Your hands need to break at just the right moment, and that allows the force of your hips and legs to transfer through your bat. Here, watch me again." Coach Allen took the stick back. He began his swing and froze. "See? I'm shining the light on the ball, then—"

Pock!

Jalen took the stick his coach offered him and tried again. "Shoot!"

"Almost. Try again."

Jalen tried but made no sound, and he studied his coach's face to see if the whole thing was a joke.

"Again," said Coach Allen, without a smile.

Jalen focused, swung, and . . .

22

POCK!

"Excellent!" Coach Allen thumped Jalen on the back. "Now you got it. I want you to take this speed hitter and swing it a hundred times a day. We are going to speed that swing up—get your lower body into it—and turn you into a monster. You'll be crushing dingers to left, right, and center.

"And when you practice with this, I want you to visualize that you're up to bat with every swing. Got that?" Coach gave him a funny look.

Jalen nodded. "Sure."

"And every swing I want you to see it end with the biggest prize a batter could wish for."

"A home run."

"Nope."

Jalen let out a small burst of laughter. He knew that he was right. "Nothing's better than a home run."

"How about a grand slam? Right?" Coach Allen tapped his skull. "That's what I want you to visualize with every swing—last inning, bases loaded, two outs, down by three, everyone on edge, and *bang!* You knock it out. Got it?"

"Like Sunday."

Coach Allen smiled and then nodded. "Like Sunday. I know, your swing was just fine. But your swing is pure instinct. If you want to connect twice as often, you have to develop repeatable technique. Hitting is all about repeating technique. All the pressure in that moment, and you still relax that swing. Got it?"

Jalen grinned and lifted the speed hitter. "Got it, Coach. Thanks."

Coach Allen checked his watch, blew his whistle, and shouted, "Okay, guys, bring it in! I have some big news!"

23

WHEN EVERYONE HAD SETTLED DOWN, COACH
said, "That was a heck of a win yesterday. And when
you win, good things happen, right? And they sure did,
because I got a phone call from Lakeland, which is this
sports academy down in Bradenton, Florida, right near
Tampa, that runs the most prestigious baseball tournaments in the country."

"My brother went to Lakeland," said Jay Katz.

Gertzy leaned over and whispered in Jalen's ear. "His
brother plays for the Dodgers low-A club."

"And, because they had a last-minute cancellation, and
because we won that tournament," Coach Allen continued, "I got a call earlier asking if we wanted to attend.

Since we were scheduled to travel this coming weekend anyway, and I spoke to one very generous parent who immediately offered to pick up the expense for everyone to fly to Florida, I have accepted Lakeland's offer."

Gertzy's grin said it all.

Coach Allen now cast a stern look at them and spread it all around before speaking. "But I don't want to do this unless you guys are ready to play to win. I don't need to go down there to work on my tan. If we go, we go to win. Deal?"

Everyone murmured, "Yes."

"Really?" Coach's mouth fell open. "That doesn't sound like you want it. Do you want it?"

"Yes!" This time it was a shout.

"Are you gonna win it?"

"YES!"

The roar sent a chill skipping down Jalen's spine.

"Good!" Coach shouted. "Tomorrow morning, practice at nine. Guys who were in the starting lineup at the end of the championship game will be with Coach Miller. The rest of you will be with me in center field."

"Coach!" Charlie Kimber raised his hand. "You want me with the starting lineup?"

Jalen paused to see what would happen.

"Were you in the lineup at the end of the championship

game in Boston?" Coach Allen stopped to scowl. Everyone else stared.

"I should have been in it." Kimber held his chin high, and Jalen couldn't help admiring the kid's guts.

"Who's the coach?" Coach Allen's face was tight.

"What do you mean?" Kimber asked.

"Who's the coach of this team?" Coach Allen was getting angrier with each word. "Are you?"

"No, sir. You are."

"And the coach decides who plays and who doesn't, right?"

"Yes, sir."

"So how could you say you were supposed to be out there?" Coach Allen spread his grim look over the entire team. "I'm here to win, guys. If you or your parents don't like it, there are plenty of other travel teams out there." He clapped his hands twice fast. "Now let's get home."

Jalen unzipped his bag at his locker. He fished around inside, felt something on his hand, and yanked it out with a bloodcurdling scream.

24

JALEN DROPPED THE BAG, BUT A SWARM OF ANGRY
spiders were already on his hand, racing up his bare arm
and into his shirtsleeve.

He beat his hand against his pants while at the same
time wriggling out of his shirt. Somehow he ended up
spinning around, tripping, and going down so that one
hand landed in the bag. He felt the spiders inside popping
like tiny grapes beneath his hand and howled again.

He shot up and whipped his shirt off, stamping it like
a burning blanket. His teammates surrounded him, going
crazy with laughter.

"Are you serious?" Jalen yelled at them.

They laughed harder.

Finally Gertzy stepped forward and shook Jalen's hand. "Welcome to the Bandits. It's official now. You got 'got.'"

"Got what?" Jalen scowled around at the grinning faces. He was surprised and super mad when he saw Daniel laughing along with the rest of them. He focused on his shirt, giving it a violent shake before tugging it on and sweeping his legs clean.

"Just 'got,' like 'Got you.' Everyone gets got. Relax. Rules are, it's got to be funny, but it can't be mean, and no one gets hurt," Gertzy said.

"I thought this team was different, a bunch of good guys pulling for each other. But on the bus, you gotta pay to use the bathroom. And you gotta watch your back every second, because even someone you like might try to poison you."

"Poison?" Gertzy wrinkled his nose.

"Spider bites are poisonous." Jalen looked up and down his arm. "I just got lucky."

"Dude, they were like the size of a penny," Gertzy said, holding his finger and thumb quite close together.

"More like a cookie." Jalen made a circle with his forefingers and thumbs.

"Whatever." Gertzy dropped his hands. "Everyone goes through it. No one gets hurt, and it's this fun thing that connects us all. No one is above getting laughed at."

"What did they do to you?" Jalen asked.

"Ha!" Gertzy said. "Frogs."

"Frogs?"

"Frogs, which they knew creep me out, in my hotel bathroom. Four in the tub, two in the sink, and after I thought they were finally all gone, one in my bed."

"That's not so bad."

"Maybe not for you. I howled like a maniac. When I was a little kid, my older brothers scared me out of my mind about frogs. They had a tree frog in their terrarium, and I think they wanted to scare me into not messing with it, so I got fed all these creepy, scary frog stories—which I no longer believe—but the damage was done. I hate frogs."

Hearing all the commotion, Coach Allen waded through the team and asked what happened.

After Gertzy explained, Coach made a sickened face. "I hate spiders. Where'd you get them?"

Fanny produced a huge empty pickle jar. There were several spiders still inside. He held it up to show off. "Took time to fill this bad boy."

"You filled it?" Coach Allen asked.

"To the brim." Fanny puffed up his chest.

Coach shook his head. "I just told you we're playing Lakeland this weekend. That is the biggest team anyone can play. This is no time for fooling around."

"But this was gonna happen before we knew," Gertzy protested.

Coach held his hand up. "I don't care when it was planned. Anything more like this before the weekend, the perpetrators get benched. Don't think it won't happen. I've got kids begging to be on the Bandits. Fanny, get Jalen's bag cleaned out."

"Me?"

"They're your spiders."

"It was Gertzy's idea." Fanny pointed at their star pitcher, and Gertzy blushed.

"It's better than peanut butter," said Gertzy with an apologetic shrug at Jalen.

Fanny peered into the bag. "I don't know. He mushed a bunch of them."

"Clean it," Coach Allen growled at Fanny. "Now."

Jalen struggled to find the right attitude. After his anger faded, he felt silly for overreacting.

"I get it," he said. "The spiders just freaked me out. How'd you know that?"

"I didn't," Gertzy said, "but who wouldn't freak out over spiders in his gear bag? Everyone knows you and me are good friends, so I couldn't take it easy on you, right?"

"I get it." Jalen tried not to grin.

25

AS FANNY BENT OVER THE BAG, HIS LOOSE PANTS
dropped a little too low on his butt.

"Hey," Daniel called out. His face twisted as if he'd smelled something gross, but no amount of control could keep him from busting out in hysterical laughter and choking on his punch line. "I hope no one's looking at my Fanny's crack!"

The team stared at Daniel in disbelief. Daniel's laughter fizzled out in his throat, and as he looked around, anger and disgust crept across his face.

"What?" he shouted. "When I say it, it's not funny?"

Damon LaClair, the team's shortstop, made a settling motion with his hands. "Dude, not cool."

"Oh, I'm not cool, huh?" Daniel shouted at the team. "All I hear is 'Fanny this' and 'Fanny that' and 'where's my farty Fanny,' but when I say one little thing, it's all of a sudden not cool!"

He turned back to Damon. "Well, you're not cool, you're a hot mess!"

Damon made a fist. "You think everything is about you and your baseball-genius buddy, but this isn't about you. It's about Coach telling us that the fooling around is over. And just so you know, we were winning championships before you two arrived, and we'll be winning them when you're gone."

Daniel made two fists and took a step toward Damon.

From the other side of the locker room, a whistle shrieked. Damon closed his eyes and took a deep breath.

Coach Allen's voice blasted as he marched their way. "You two got time to chat? I know you don't have time to fight. But anyone on this team would know that if he wanted to stay on this team, he sure as heck isn't even dreaming about fighting! Okay, get out on the field! Single file behind Kimber! EVERYONE! Lap the field, and don't stop until I say so, and you better not loaf when you're sprinting to the front of the line! That'd be a good way to get yourself out of the starting lineup! If you quit when practice gets hard, you'll quit when a game gets hard too!"

Without hesitation, the players filed outside. The only sound was the clack of their cleats against the floor. Before long they were stretched into a broken line of stragglers as the running took its toll on their hearts and minds. Jalen was just in front of Daniel, so he heard the curses uttered by the kids who passed him in a sprint.

They ran until Fanny broke ranks, hugged the trash can, and puked his guts out.

Fanny looked up from the trash can as Jalen walked past, down the first base line. On Fanny's lower lip, suspended from a string of acid drool, hung a chunk of hot dog like a little jewel on a pendant. "What are you looking at, genius?"

Jalen tasted the sour brew from his own stomach involuntarily creeping into his throat, and he dry-heaved as he looked away.

26

AFTER THE RUN, DANIEL AND JALEN DECLINED
Gertzy's peace offering to meet the team at the Häagen-Dazs, like they had after last Friday's practice.

"Catch you later," Jalen mumbled to Gertzy, following Daniel outside to the waiting pickup. When they were opening the truck doors, Jalen asked Daniel if he was sure he didn't want to join the team for ice cream. Daniel replied with a bitter, "No."

Daniel's father must have been looking forward to another dulce de leche. He gave Daniel a funny look from his seat high up in the truck.

"I got a headache," Daniel explained as he climbed in. "Besides, I'm sick of all their rules: 'say this,' 'don't say that,' 'do this,' 'don't do that.' It's hot sauce, if you ask me. Can everybody take a joke, or can't they? Me? I can take a joke. Them? They can take their Peanut Butter Salted Fudge and shove it. I'm so sick of phonies," he grumbled from the front seat. But, like Jalen's mother said about his father, Daniel never could stay mad long.

"Besides, now I've got to wait to get it like you did. You heard Coach. I wanted to get it over with tomorrow!"

"Uh . . . so you're okay with it?" Jalen knew he'd gotten way too upset by the prank.

Daniel snorted. "You think I'm afraid of some spiders or frogs? Snakes? They put a snake in my bag, I just might chomp its head off. You ever see that video of Liam Grover swallowing a lizard? I could do that too. It's the pro thing to do. Ha! Imagine the looks on their faces then."

"That's great."

"Yeah, my middle name is disgusting." Daniel twisted around in his seat up front. "Amigo, they got the wrong guy."

"For sure. You'll laugh it off and you won't miss a beat."

"Darn straight," Daniel said. "Hey—what's that YouTube video doing?"

"Only fifty more views. It's circling the bowl."

"Hot sauce!" Daniel said Cat was a genius for telling

them not to worry. "She knows things. And she knows how to do things too."

"Yeah, she's the best." The way Daniel looked at him made Jalen wish he could take it back.

Daniel turned to face the road. "Hey, I know you like her. You can't fool your amigo."

Jalen had to laugh. They'd all been best friends for so long. "Yeah, you've got my number."

He was going to text Cat about the video when a message came in from his mom.

Did you tell your dad yet?

"No," Jalen barked aloud, "I didn't!"

Daniel spun around and his dad cast a nervous glance in the mirror.

"I . . ." Jalen held up his phone. "Not you guys. I was talking out loud about this text."

Daniel covered for him. "My amigo is shaken up. You should've seen his face. Fanny put spiders in his bag. I'm talking, like, thousands. He reached right in and my man did a dance and fell right into them."

"Hey, I'll get over it!" Jalen paused. "Actually, I think I need some air. Do you mind dropping me close to the diner?"

After Daniel's dad dropped him off in the center of town, Jalen walked toward the Silver Liner. As he got close, he felt the urge to just march inside and blurt it out to his dad, but even the idea embarrassed him. He felt like he had betrayed his father on two counts—the video and his mom—at the exact time when everything was going perfectly with his dad's restaurant. So Jalen kept walking.

27

LATE AFTERNOON SUNSHINE POURED DOWN FROM above, baking the gravel driveway and exciting the locusts and bullfrogs in the wetlands on either side. The end loop of the driveway was just inside the woods. Jalen strode into the cool cave of shade, enjoying the whisper of the trees. Suddenly home didn't look as awful as he'd come to think. Inside, he was struck not by the crooked walls, but by the comfort of the sagging couch that he always fell asleep on. His father's big chair that leaked its stuffing from a split seam . . .

Jalen knew he was crying and fought to pull himself together. Baseball, that was what he wanted to think about, not how to tell his dad about his mom's sudden appearance.

He sat down at the kitchen table to eat leftover lasagna, with a can of orange soda and his iPhone. He googled Lakeland, and an entirely unexpected new world opened up. It was even better than Gertzy had made it sound. Lakeland wasn't like a sports camp; it looked like a sports country.

They coached future pros in everything from baseball and football to tennis, golf, and lacrosse. They had incredible training facilities and a five-thousand-seat park for football tournaments and track-and-field meets. They were so big that they had a world-class hotel on the grounds for parents, scouts, and other visitors.

You could go to a camp for five weeks, or you could live there and go to school from sixth grade until you graduated from their high school. It was all so incredible.

Jalen surfed to a Wikipedia page that listed Lakeland Academy high school graduates. The pro training alumni page was full of MLB MVPs: Gary Sheffield, Joe Mauer, Joey Votto, Andrew McCutchen. . . .

The name Andrew McCutchen stopped him.

Jalen was too young to have seen him in his MVP-level years with the Pirates, but McCutchen had been a Yankee for half a season before getting a big free-agent contract with the Phillies. Cutch had been a real fireplug, a leadoff hitter with a great batting eye. His incredible plate discipline and situational hitting skill made him a difference maker for the offense.

He was also one of the very few African American stars in MLB, a player universally liked for his effort and energy and leadership. Cutch was somebody people rooted for, and Jalen wanted to be like him.

Another look at Lakeland's website informed him that tuition for training and high school was over $72,000 a year. Jalen's balloon burst. So much money! And even if the Silver Liner franchise business took off and they were rolling in cash, there was no way his dad would want Jalen to live far away. And Jalen didn't want that either. It wouldn't be fair, anyway. It would make his father unhappy, just when the Silver Liner was becoming a success.

But Lakeland was also the best of the best. If Jalen could dominate this tournament, maybe he'd have a shot at one of their scholarships.

Which was more important, he asked himself: being true and loyal and living with Dad . . . or taking his big chance to follow his MLB dream?

It made him sick inside to realize that both were equally important.

28

BECAUSE THEIR OLD SET WAS SO BAD, JALEN
wasn't in the habit of watching much TV. Trying to ease
his mind, he flopped between playing *Clash* and thinking about baseball until he remembered the speed hitter
Coach Allen had given him. He went outside and began to
swing. Jalen could easily imagine a stadium packed with
fans. He did as his coach told him and conjured up a game
on the line in need of a grand slam.

Over and over he swung. At first he muffed it. He slowed
down and began to relax. Soon he filled the empty house
with solid thwacking—the sound of success. He worked
up another sweat before jumping into the shower.

Lying on his bed, he took up his phone to study the text

his mom had sent. In his mind he planned to message Cat about Lakeland, but he was suddenly exhausted. The hand with the phone wilted down onto the mattress, and despite all the unanswered questions in his mind, he was pulled down into a deeply troubled sleep.

Sunshine blinked through the leaves and through the window, waking Jalen up early. Next door, his father was still snoring. Jalen stood at his dad's bedroom door, watching the rise and fall of his father's chest. He'd fallen asleep in his short-sleeved black scrubs, with his arms folded across his chest. He was still wearing his glasses.

Drawing closer, Jalen wanted to shake his father awake and tell him she was here. Get it over with. He was reaching out to touch his arm when his dad let out a snort. Without opening his eyes, he rolled over, settled on his side, and continued to snore. He must have come in extra late and exhausted.

Jalen tiptoed to the bathroom. When he'd finished, he peeked in again, but his dad was still sleeping soundly. Jalen decided to leave him alone. He suspected Cat would give him grief, but that was better than telling his dad that his mom and her "partner" were in town. He was sure his dad would be hurt by that—and by the fact that Jalen had secretly hired a detective to find her.

On the kitchen table, a white paper bag was filled with leftovers from the restaurant: crusty bread, butter, and one of his favorites, three-cheese bellflower pasta, was in the fridge.

His dad thought using a microwave to reheat food was uncivilized, but Jalen used it anyway. It whirred for a few minutes, then beeped. The pasta was steaming. While Jalen ate carefully to avoid burning his mouth, he checked for the video. The viewers had almost stopped coming.

Jalen shook his head. Something he thought was going to be a real nightmare was less threatening every time he looked, and something he thought would be a dream come true had given him nightmares.

His dad was still sleeping when he let himself out the door and walked to the Silver Liner. Greta was already inside, scrubbing table seven with a sponge.

"Late night last night?" Jalen said to make conversation.

"Why your father hired these so-called cleaners I'll never know," she replied, working up a lather with the sponge.

"Didn't he do it to help you?"

"Come here. Look at this." She pointed a purple-painted pinky nail at a dried spaghetti string. "You call this clean?"

"Yeah, but won't that get covered by the tablecloth?"

"And you think that's good enough?" Greta put her hand on her hip. "Hiding the dirt isn't the same as clean, Ace."

Jalen wanted to shortcut the lecture. "Yeah, I guess."

"You guess?"

Luckily, his phone rang. "Oh, it's JY. I gotta take this."

He put the phone to his ear and marched outside.

Even Greta knew that when JY called, you answered.

29

JALEN MUTTERED INTO THE PHONE, "SAVED BY
the bell."

"Saved from what?" asked the Yankees star.

Jalen waited until he was out the door. "Well, first,
Greta's cleanliness speech. But—great news—the video
isn't getting views!"

JY had news of his own. "Reuben Hall's wife went into
labor early this morning, so I'm playing in the first game
of the doubleheader today. I'm hoping you can give me a
hand after all. The game's at one. I already spoke to Tory,
and you're all set with a ride. I got seats in the owner's
box, so you'll be sitting where you normally do."

Jalen had been in the front row right by the Yankees

dugout before. The view of the pitcher was perfect.

"That's great news, right?" Jalen asked. "You thought being a Yankee was over."

JY took a moment before he spoke, and Jalen could hear the two Rottweilers barking somewhere in the distant background. "This isn't a vote of confidence. It's just a guy's wife having a baby."

"Oh."

"Yeah, Chan is starting, so I have to wonder if that has something to do with it too." JY sounded like he was talking to himself.

"Wait! You didn't get to hear about my dad! The Yankees want a Silver Liner Diner in the mezzanine."

"Your diner on the mezzanine? That's a game changer!" JY's voice took on new determination. "They can't trade me now. And today I'll show them why they don't want to!"

Jalen's mind immediately flooded with numbers, statistics he'd seen on Jake Chan's pitching. They were right there, clear as a colossal billboard. "Chan has a terrific slider-and-changeup combo. They're his best swing-and-miss pitches, set up by an average fastball."

"They're not so great if you know they're coming and can pass on them. And the good news is," JY said, "that if Foxx doesn't keep his word and re-sign me, I'll have a shot at getting picked up by another team. The Red Sox game alone showed everyone I've still got some mojo. If I do well today, Tory says it'll help even more."

"Anyway, who's Tory?" Jalen scuffed some grit beneath his shoes. He was miffed that JY hadn't mentioned him when he talked about mojo.

"You know. Victoria. Hello. Cat's mom?"

"You call her Tory?"

"Is that okay with you?" JY's voice was harsh.

Jalen wanted to say that he knew one person who would mind, and that was Cat, but he kicked a rock and said, "Sure. Fine. Just asking."

"Good. She and Cat will pick you up at eleven thirty."

Jalen hesitated. "Can I bring Gertzy?"

"Who's Gertzy?"

"My friend. He's our ace pitcher."

"Sure. Why not?" JY said. "There's four tickets, so you can bring a friend." He suddenly refocused on the news. "The Silver Liner at the stadium. People will go nuts. Your dad will get rich." He laughed. "Who would have guessed that calamari was so lucky!"

"Thanks to you," Jalen said. "Hey, maybe you could do another tweet tonight, after the game?"

"Sure." JY said. "Let's make sure I've got something to brag about first, though, right?"

"I haven't failed you yet, have I?" Jalen flexed his arm, admiring the shadow his bicep made on the parking lot.

"No. You have not."

Jalen's heart swelled with pride, but after they'd hung up their phones, his mind swirled inside a tornado of thoughts and feelings about his mom, his dad, Cat, JY, and now Daniel. What was he doing? Thinking of Gertzy before Daniel? Not telling his father?

Jalen knew that he'd have to talk to Daniel before he invited Gertzy to the game. He dreaded making the call but knew he had to. He would tell Daniel that he'd invite Gertzy only if it was okay with him.

He squinted from the glare of the sun as he dialed Daniel's number.

30

"S'UP?" DANIEL SOUNDED SLEEPY.

"Hey, amigo, you're not gonna believe this."

Daniel yawned. "Try me."

"JY is playing in the early game of the doubleheader today," Jalen said. "He wants my help."

"Awesome, amigo. We in the owner's seats again?" Daniel sounded awake now, and his excitement made Jalen's stomach clench and roll.

"Uh, no. Close by, though," Jalen said.

"Who's on the mou— Oh, hot sauce!"

"What's wrong?" Jalen asked. "Why hot sauce?"

"Because my dad is taking my mom to the city, and I'm watching my sister all afternoon."

"Aw, that's too bad."

The silence stretched out between them. With a secret sigh of relief, Jalen imagined the grin on Gertzy's face when they sat down in those prime seats and ordered food for free off a menu card, real VIP treatment.

Then Daniel said, "Wait a minute. I know. I'll ask my mom if my sister can go with them! I'll call you back."

Before Jalen could speak, he was disconnected.

He looked at his phone before stuffing it in his pocket and hustling back inside the restaurant. He restocked the San Marzano tomatoes his dad used to make his special sauces. Then he filled different shakers with salt, black pepper, and red pepper and put them on the counter and tables in the dining area.

When he finished up, he said, "Greta, I have to go get ready. Dad's probably still passed out and I don't want to wake him. Would you tell him JY's playing in the first game of the doubleheader, and I've got to be there? I'm going home to get my stuff. I'll go straight to my own practice afterward."

Greta said, "You go do your thing! If it wasn't for you and JY, I'd be wearing a dirty apron and serving greasy cheeseburgers past midnight."

Jalen smiled. It felt good to be appreciated. "Thanks, Greta."

He was heading toward the door and Greta was asking whether he could get any more cute, single Yankees players interested in calamari when his phone rang.

It was Daniel.

31

JALEN SAID, "HEY."

"It's hot sauce, amigo. Burning red-hot sauce."

Jalen skipped down the steps. "Aw, that stinks."

"My dad said I could go, yeah, but that if I did, then I'd have to babysit my sister tonight because if they have her all afternoon"—Daniel heaved a sigh—"then he's gonna take my mom out to dinner tonight. 'It's your choice,' he said. Yeah, some choice. Then I miss practice right when I'm on the coach's radar. Thanks for nothing."

"Coach Allen might be okay."

"I'm not you, amigo," Daniel said.

"You're a great reliever . . . and a pretty good fielder, too," Jalen said, hurrying along.

Daniel brightened. "I did help bring in the win Sunday."

Jalen was walking faster. "Hey, amigo, I gotta go get ready. I'll meet you there tonight. Cat's mom will drop me off after the game."

"Knock 'em dead, amigo."

Jalen dialed up Cat. "Hey, Cat. You heard about JY, right?"

"Yeah, I've been waiting for your call," she said. "Did you talk to Daniel?"

"I did. He has to watch his sister."

"Oh, hot sauce," Cat replied.

"That's what he said. Hey, Cat, I was thinking that since we've got four tickets, and there's no sense wasting one, I could invite Gertzy. He's a great kid, and I know your mom will love him."

"Sure," Cat said. "You know my mom."

"And maybe we can pick him up?"

"Sounds good. We'll pick you up at eleven thirty," she said. "You feeling good? Got the magic?"

"Oh yeah. Magic is at DEFCON one."

"Ha-ha. That's it," Cat said. "See you soon."

Jalen hung up and slowed down. He dialed Gertzy, got voice mail, hung up, and texted him, asking if he wanted to go to the afternoon Yankees game and sit by the dugout as JY's guests.

Gertzy replied immediately.

Does a bear poop in the woods?

Jalen grinned.

Pick you up. Where?

When the address came, Jalen forwarded it to Cat, then walked through the trees to his house. A big yellow truck was backing out of the driveway, and his father was waving good-bye to the men inside.

"Jalen," he shouted. "You're here!"

"Dad, I thought you were sleeping."

"Who needs the sleep? Come with me!"

Jalen followed his dad into the living room and was surprised to see a huge TV that filled the wall.

"Is for you and me." His father beamed with delight. "We gonna watch the Yankees, and the World Cup, and any movies you like."

"Wow, Dad. Awesome." Jalen hugged his father tight.

Jalen felt like it was the perfect moment to talk about his dream: his mom.

He stood back to speak.

But then Jalen's dad said, "Well, is all because of you and JY. You make my dream come true."

His dad's happiness stopped him.

Jalen stammered, then said, "Yeah, but you're the one with the lucky calamari, Dad."

Jalen's dad clasped his shoulder and squeezed it several times.

Jalen started talking about JY and the afternoon game.

"You gonna make him win! Now I gotta get to the Sliver Liner and cook."

Jalen set his equipment bag on the edge of the driveway as his dad pulled away in the van. He realized he'd been holding his breath. He'd missed the chance to talk about his mom. Again.

Frustrated, he dug the new speed hitter out of his bag and began to swing.

"What are you?" he asked himself with a grunt. "A total wimp?"

Jalen envisioned the loaded bases, the two outs, and the full count in the final inning, with his team down by three. He swung and missed the timing. He reset the image and swung for the grand slam again. He missed again, then swung over and over. He worked himself into a furious sweat without once hearing the sound he was trying for. Finally he bounced the stick off the gravel. It rolled at an angle, stopping at the grass. He kicked it and stubbed his toe on a rock.

"Oh, farts!" he screamed to let off steam.

Jalen danced around on one foot, losing his cap. He

bent to pick it up and heard a vehicle pull into the drive-way. The Range Rover's window went down.

"You good?" Cat asked.

"Fine." Jalen tossed his gear in back and got in. "Thanks for doing this, Mrs. H."

Cat's mom backed out of the driveway and said, "JY needs his fans."

Cat turned around in her seat to look at him. "So, you ready for this?"

"Does a bear p— eat in the woods?" Jalen said.

Cat scowled at him and flashed her eyes at her mom. "Really? Bear pee?"

"No, I said 'eat.' It just came out wrong. Sorry."

Cat waved a hand in the air. "Oh. Yeah. Sorry. I'm just jumpy."

"Why are you jumpy?" Jalen asked.

"What if JY doesn't get the contract that that slime ball Foxx promised he'd get?"

"Language, Catrina!" Mrs. H sounded angry, but her next words made Jalen hide a smile. "'Creep' is less vul-gar and just as good."

"How can you get paid if JY gets traded or released? And what does that do to the Silver Liner?"

A chill gripped Jalen. He had big plans for that money: among other things, a car for when he could drive, and college. "But Foxx already went on record. He told the media that if JY batted a thousand in those games two weeks ago, he'd give him a new contract."

Cat faced the road. "Can you name anyone more likely to lie than Jeffrey Foxx?"

They rode in silence for a bit before Jalen said, "Nope."

Cat turned around again so she could look him in the eyes. "That's why I'm jumpy. If we ever needed you to be a baseball genius, now is the time."

"Oh," he said. "Okay."

"Oh, c'mon! That didn't sound like confidence." Cat reminded him of Coach Allen. "Are you gonna be ready to do this?"

32

JALEN HESITATED ONLY A MOMENT. "DOES A BEAR eat in the woods?"

She grinned, and gave him knuckles.

Gertzy was in his curving driveway, shooting baskets. His long jump shot got nothing but net, and he set the ball on the lawn before hoisting his gear bag from the back hatch of a Mercedes SUV. The house wasn't as big as the mansion Cat lived in, but it rivaled JY's place for sure. Gertzy's mom came out to meet Cat's mom before they set out for Yankee Stadium.

The three friends started talking baseball, giving opinions about the problems the Orioles could create and the answers the Yankees might have.

"Wait till you see Jalen solve Jake Chan like a Rubik's Cube," Cat said.

"I saw him do it to Chris Gamble, but doing it to a big-league pitcher in Yankee Stadium?" Gertzy said, leaning closer to Cat. "This is gonna be awesome."

They got off the expressway, slowing down in some traffic before taking a turn into a closed street. Mrs. H held up a pass on her dash, and a police officer waved them through. She cruised to the garage near Gate 2 and parked.

Jalen then led them proudly into the Legends Suite club, where they ordered complimentary food from an almost endless menu of choices. From there they went up into the stadium.

Jalen could feel people's eyes on him. One man grabbed his son and said, "Look, it's the Calamari Kid." The air was warm, but the windy sky above swelled with gray clouds that seemed to promise rain. Maybe the weather was the reason there was just a small crowd, or maybe it was the afternoon time. Jalen could feel the lack of buzz in the air. It dampened the thrill he had enjoyed other times he'd come to help JY. Cat's mom gave the usher their tickets, and he passed them through with a smile.

The owner's box, right up against the low concrete wall with only dirt between them and home plate, had a lot of empty seats. There might have been room for Daniel, and

Jalen kicked himself for not asking if he could bring three friends, but then he remembered Daniel's sister and he felt better.

Gertzy hustled to sit next to Cat. Jalen frowned, taking a seat on her other side, putting Mrs. H on the aisle.

"Man, are you livin' right," said Gertzy. "I can't wait until the food comes."

Jalen bit the inside of his cheek. "It's not bad, is it?"

They all stood for the national anthem. JY turned back toward them from his spot on the right field line, giving them a smile and a discreet wave before heading out to second base.

"Are you kidding?" Gertzy said under his breath to Jalen. "James Yager just waved at us."

"Yeah," Jalen said.

The way Gertzy looked at him made Jalen feel proud, but the way he kept looking at Cat gave Jalen a twinge. Their food came. The game had started, but watching what was going on between his friends, Jalen had a hard time concentrating.

In the top of the first, there was one out and an Orioles runner on first when JY electrified the thin crowd with a leaping grab of a soft liner and a rocket throw to first to complete a double play.

JY tipped his cap to the cheering fans as he jogged

toward the dugout. When he winked at Jalen before disappearing down the stairs, Jalen knew he had to grow up and be like JY. He had to have a big crowd—thousands of admirers—cheering for him.

The Orioles took the field. Jalen studied Jake Chan on the mound. Chan was no "surefire" thing. Drafted in the thirty-sixth round after high school, he went to college and shot up to only the eleventh round. After four years in the minors, he developed a fastball-slider-changeup repertoire good enough to make the all-star team.

Switch-hitting Aaron Hicks led off, only to punch out chasing a sharply breaking slider that nearly hit him on the back foot.

"Holy cow, I wish I could throw a pitch that breaks like that," Gertzy said.

"You got it yet?" Cat asked Jalen.

"I've only seen five pitches, Cat. And he scrapped his windup. His throwing every pitch from the stretch complicates things."

"I know, but sometimes . . ." Cat's voice faded away.

"How's it work?" Gertzy asked, quickly back with the program.

"It's hard to explain," Jalen said. "I have all these numbers in my head, stats, even from the minor leagues. Then I just clear my mind and watch the pitcher. Sometimes it takes five or six pitches, sometimes it never happens. Mostly, it takes around ten or twelve, and I just feel it."

"That's so sick," Gertzy said.

Jalen only nodded. Aaron Judge was at the plate, and Chan was studying him. Jalen tried to keep his focus on Chan, but his eyes kept straying to Judge's stance. The man was a phenomenal hitter with great plate discipline. Jalen wanted to get that kind of reputation.

Chan threw a four-seam heater low inside. Judge let it go, stepped back, and turned to see the umpire make a punching motion and call a strike. Because his six-foot-seven height was so hard for umps to adjust for, Judge got more low pitches called strikes than any other player in MLB. He gave the ump a quizzical shrug before stepping back into the box.

Chan threw a curve next and Judge nicked it foul.

"Here comes that slider," Jalen said.

Chan wound up and threw what looked like a fastball until the last instant, when the ball cut down and across the plate and out of the strike zone. Judge swung but the ball only dribbled to the second baseman, who made the easy toss to first for the out.

Gertzy reached across Cat for a fist bump. "You did it. You got this now, right?"

33

"I THINK," JALEN SAID.

"Sweet," said Gertzy.

Jalen wanted to explain that one correct call didn't mean he had his groove. In fact, it could have been a lucky guess. But he wanted to impress Gertzy, so he said nothing more.

Tyler Hutt was up next. As the Yankees batter stepped into the box, Jalen said, "Fastball."

Chan threw a fastball that Hutt got ahold of and bounced off the left-field wall for a double.

"My man!" Gertzy high-fived Jalen and Cat. "That's what I'm talking about!"

Spencer Tollis left the on-deck circle and approached

the right-hand batter's box. Jalen was on a roll, but he still didn't feel it the way he should if he were really dialed in. He thought Chan would throw a sinker—his least-used pitch—but he didn't know for sure.

"Curve," he said instead, a moment before Chan wound up.

Tollis's time was off on what appeared to be a four-seam fastball coming out of Chan's hand, but was actually a slow breaker. Tollis got wood on the ball, but it bounced weakly before landing in Chan's mitt, making the throw to first an easy out.

"Did you see that filth?" Gertzy was so excited, he jumped out of his seat.

"Easy, Gertzy," said Cat. "We're Yankees fans, remember?"

Gertzy looked around them at all the frowning faces and melted into his seat. "Oh yeah. Sorry." He busied himself with his smoothie.

Cat leaned toward Jalen. "You got it now, huh?"

"I think."

"You said that before, but you called the last three pitches," said Cat.

"I guess I like to play this safe," Jalen said.

Top of the second, and the Yankees were out in the field again. From second base JY gave Jalen a thumbs-up signal right after a thumbs-down. Jalen answered JY's questioning look by holding his hand sideways with his thumb out and waggling it up and down, signaling *maybe*. He could see the frustration on JY's face, but he knew better than to guess. JY had strictly forbidden it.

To make matters worse, JY made a wild throw to third base that allowed a runner to score before Tanaka struck out his third batter, ending the half inning. JY jogged into the dugout and emerged wearing batting gloves and helmet. He took his spot in the on-deck circle with Greg Gonzalez, his lips clamped tight and looking grim.

Jalen tried to ignore him and instead focus on Chan as he threw a handful of warm-up pitches. When Torres dug in, Jalen knew Chan would start him off with a fastball but didn't say it out loud.

"What do you think?" asked Gertzy.

"I gotta concentrate, Gertzy." The words sounded sharper than Jalen intended. When the phone buzzed in his pocket, he hit ignore without looking. He was trying to focus entirely on the Orioles pitcher.

Chan shook off whatever the catcher signaled, then gave a nod and wound up before throwing what had to be a fastball, only it wasn't. The pitch was thrown to look like a fastball but was noticeably slower, a changeup. Unfortunately for Chan, his changeup had no downward tilt. It floated in the strike zone rather than dropping out of it.

Gonzalez launched that cement-mixer pitch into the left-field seats. The few fans there jumped to their feet and roared.

JY was up to bat, and Jalen was shaken. His phone buzzed insistently and he wrenched it from his pocket to turn it off. Gonzalez was soaking up the cheers and taking his time rounding the bases. When Jalen saw that the caller was his mom, he answered without thinking.

"Mom?"

"Oh, Jalen. I'm sorry to bother you, but I'm so excited." She was nearly breathless.

"About what?" Jalen asked.

"Well, it was George's idea, really." Her laughter danced through the phone. "Jalen, we figured out how to tell your father about me!"

Jalen froze. Were they at the Silver Liner?

34

CAT GRABBED HIS ARM, PULLING HIM BACK TO the game.

JY tossed the weighted bat doughnut on the ground and gave Jalen a look of hope before marching toward the plate.

"Mom," he said quickly, "I can't talk now. I'll call you back?"

"Of course! I'm sorry, I didn't mean to pester you." She sounded hurt. "You're busy, and here I am . . ."

JY took a couple of practice swings outside the batter's box, but his eyes were on Jalen.

"I gotta go!" He disconnected his mom.

He thought Chan would throw a fastball, but he wasn't

sure of the pitch and could only offer JY a weak shrug of apology. When Chan threw a slider, he knew he'd done the right thing, even though JY had swung and missed. Cat saw the look that JY gave Jalen, and she squeezed his hand.

"It's not the first time I haven't been zoned in during his first at bat." Jalen was talking as much to himself as to Cat.

"Maybe it'll come to you while he's still up," Cat said hopefully.

"Maybe." Jalen had his eyes glued to the pitcher, but his mind was on his mom.

He thought slider again, but Chan threw a four-seam fastball inside. JY let it by. When the umpire called a strike, JY stepped back and howled. Jalen knew the theatrics were to give him time to figure things out, but he was no closer to knowing the pitches. In truth, he was still shaken by his mother's call.

JY let the next pitch go, a changeup in the dirt. On the 1–2 count he swung at and missed a slider that broke sideways and down. He retired to the dugout without so much as a glance at Jalen.

"It's okay." Cat patted his leg, then leaned over to Gertzy. "Sometimes it takes a little longer."

"Oh, I know he can do it. He did it for me on Sunday."

Gertzy spoke with as much enthusiasm as Daniel ever had, and that comforted Jalen.

Jalen turned his attention back to Chan. The Orioles pitcher struck out the next two Yankees batters with pitch sequences featuring a frustrating mix of heat and unhittable off-speed pitches, but still Jalen was no closer to an answer.

Inning over, he turned to Cat and told her about the call from his mom.

"You didn't sound rude at all to me," Cat said.

"Yeah, but I just hung up on her."

"Well," Cat said, "call her back. You're going to be distracted until you do, and the Orioles are up anyway."

Jalen pressed his lips tight but nodded in agreement. He excused himself, found a quiet corner in the VIP lounge, and called his mom.

"Hello?" she said.

"Hi, Mom."

"Hi."

"I'm really sorry about that. I'm at Yankee Stadium and I'm having a hard time," he said.

"Oh, I said I never wanted to bother you, and I meant that. I wasn't saying it willy-nilly," she said.

Jalen looked at the clock on his phone. "I've got to get back for the next inning, but I felt bad and wanted you to know that we can talk later about how to tell Dad. Okay?"

"That's fine, Jalen. Whenever you want, son. I only want to help. Just know I'll be busy tonight. I'm singing at the Jazz Forum!"

Jalen felt a sudden hope. The fear that his mom—and George—had gone to the Silver Liner without him was gone. Worry had made it impossible for what Cat and Daniel called his baseball genius to work. Maybe now he could get back to the game and do what he'd come to do.

"Thank you, Mom," he said. "You're awesome."

There was silence at the other end of the connection, and when his mom finally spoke, her voice trembled with emotion. "I'm hardly awesome, Jalen."

"You are to me." It was the nicest thing he could think of, and she rewarded him with a happy sigh.

Back outside, he saw the Orioles had added another run and there were runners on first and third with only one out. Chris Davis topped a Tanaka curveball, driving it into the grass halfway to the pitcher's mound and sending it high over second base. With incredible quickness, JY bolted underneath the ball, made a barehanded grab, and flicked it to Gonzalez, who was covering second. Gonzalez also snatched the ball barehanded and made a red-hot throw to first for the second double play of the game.

The crowd went wild, including Jalen and his friends.

Gertzy high-fived Jalen and Cat. "He's still got the mojo. He's still JY! What? You don't think so, Jalen?"

Jalen realized he'd been frowning. "If JY's gonna fend off Foxx and stay with the Yankees, he needs his bat to be as good as his glove."

"That's where you come in, buddy." Gertzy patted him on his shoulder.

"Yeah," Jalen said. "That's where I come in."

Darker clouds massed above the stadium. The warm breeze whispered the promise of rain. Jalen wondered if a rainout might not be the best thing that could happen, but he also remembered seeing a forecast that said the front wasn't due till midnight.

He tried to clear his mind. He needed to be ready. He ate some nachos and began working on a hot dog while he watched Chan shut down the bottom of the Yankees lineup. As the Yankees took the field, Cat asked, "How you feeling?"

"Like I'm almost there," he said.

Unfortunately, Jalen wasn't almost there. Far from it.

The situation with his mom would not quit haunting Jalen. The Yankees cycled through the entire lineup twice, and then some, with JY striking out twice, before Jalen bolted upright in his seat and said, "I got it."

"You got it?" Cat clapped her hands repeatedly.

"You got it?" Gertzy bumped knuckles with Jalen.

Jalen couldn't wait to signal JY, but the inning ended before JY was up, and he didn't look Jalen's way once while he was in the field.

It was the top of the seventh inning. The score was tied at 4–4 and there were two outs before Hanser Alberto saw a split-finger fastball with no life. He went yard on Tanaka with runners on second and third, giving the Orioles a 7–4 lead. The Yankees sent Chris Pagonis to the mound, and he methodically struck out the next batter.

Chan was still on the mound for the Orioles, and Gonzalez was up. JY looked grim in the on-deck circle until he saw Jalen give him a thumbs-up. JY seemed to swing with more purpose, and even though Gonzalez grounded out, JY approached the plate with his shoulders straight and his head high.

Jalen looked at Chan briefly, then signaled fastball to JY. The ballplayer stepped up to the plate. Chan wound up.

Jalen closed his eyes.

35

THE CRACK OF JY'S BAT SMASHED THE SILENCE.
He'd crushed one.

Jalen's eyes popped open in time to watch the baseball sail over the left-field fence and get swallowed up by the stands. All four of them, including Cat's mom, flew out of their seats, cheering as JY rounded the bases.

"That's two dingers in two games!" Cat hollered as she slapped everyone high fives.

Gertzy hugged Jalen. "Unbelievable!"

JY tipped his cap to the crowd and enjoyed the slaps from his teammates, but he didn't disappear into the dugout before rewarding Jalen with a wink and a smile. Jalen pumped a fist in the air, returning the show of teeth, until he realized what the Orioles were doing behind the backs of the celebratory Bronx Bombers.

The Orioles manager, Brandon Hyde, took the ball from a stoic Chan and waited for relief from the bull pen.

"I guess be careful what you wish for," Jalen muttered.

Cat wrinkled her nose. "What do you mean?"

"That home run ended Chan's day," Jalen said, "and now I've got to start all over."

Gertzy squinted at the Orioles dugout. "Do you know who that even is?"

"Unfortunately, I do." Jalen sighed.

"Who? He's like seven feet high."

"Close," Jalen said. "It's Mick Connor. He's six foot seven, and he's got a killer sinker."

The three friends stared as the Orioles relief pitcher warmed up.

"Look at that funky release," Cat said.

"Looks like a catapult," said Gertzy.

"He throws that sinker ninety-seven miles per hour." Jalen removed his Yankees cap and scratched his head. "If that wasn't enough, he throws a slider out of the same arm tunnel."

Gertzy swallowed a mouthful of smoothie. "What else has he got?"

"That's really it." Jalen turned his attention to Castro.

"He's got a changeup, but only for lefties."

"Won't that make it easier to figure him out?" Cat asked. "With only two pitches, I mean?"

Jalen shrugged and shook his head. "No idea."

JY also knew what a new pitcher meant. He turned to make eye contact with Jalen as he left the dugout at the tops of the eighth and ninth innings. By the bottom of the ninth, the Yankees were still down 7–5, and a late rally against Connor seemed unlikely.

The bottom of the ninth prompted another Baltimore pitching change. The O's were working with a "closer by committee" approach, so Jalen discovered who was pitching the bottom of the ninth when the bull-pen gate opened and Jonathan Harris trotted toward the mound.

"I hope you're up for a challenge again," Cat said with a chirpy brightness.

"What's he got?" Gertzy asked.

Accessing his mental data banks, Jalen said, "Three out of four pitches are ninety-five-plus fastballs, and the rest are an even split between sliders and changeups. With smart sequencing, he can tie batters in knots."

An admiring "Wow" was all Gertzy had to say.

After eight warm-up pitches that Jalen watched trance-like, Harris punched out Aaron Hicks on three balls and three strikes.

"Harris has a feel for it now," Jalen said.

"Yeah, but do you?" Cat asked.

Tollis approached the plate. He passed on a high fastball, and then Harris fell apart. The next pitch hit the dirt, got by the catcher, and allowed Hutt to steal second. The fans began a low murmur. After Tollis walked on four pitches, Baltimore's pitching coach jogged to the mound. He gave Harris a confidence-boosting talk, probably suggesting pitches too.

Jalen groaned. "How can I know what Harris is going to throw if he doesn't know?"

"But we could win this," Cat said.

"No thanks to me if we do, I'm afraid. Plus, I've got just one batter to figure him out."

"But you've got to try," Cat said.

"I will, Cat. I'll try. I don't want to leave JY hanging."

Cat smiled and patted his arm. "Just relax and do your best."

"Gonzalez can load the bases," said Gertzy. "Then JY will walk the game off with a double, or better . . . a grand slam. This is so dope."

Jalen's heart pounded against the inside of his chest. He breathed deeply and tried to empty his mind.

Gonzalez dug into the box and whiffed on the first heater, high and inside.

"That was some fastball," Gertzy said.

Jalen watched JY in the circle, calmly swinging his bat.

"Crazy." Gertzy stuffed some popcorn into his face like he was watching a horror movie.

Jalen shook his head, trying to clear his mind. At least Daniel knew enough not to make distractions when he was trying to read a pitcher.

The next pitch was another fastball, low and away. Gonzalez let it by for a 1–1 count. Harris then shook off his catcher twice before nodding and throwing an outrageous dipping changeup that Gonzalez chased and missed by two feet. Harris pumped a fist and turned around. When he topped the mound, Jalen said, "Another fastball."

"What did you say?" Cat's eyes widened.

Jalen glanced at her, his legs jiggling, as Harris wound up. The ball came in knee-high on a rope. Gonzalez swung down at the fastball and connected. He topped the ball into the dirt in front of home plate, and it bounced over the mound. Gonzalez took off, but topspin brought the ball down. He'd never make it safe to first base.

The second baseman, wearing a huge grin, got under it and snapped it up like a pop fly.

Time froze for an almost unbelievable moment.

Then all the Orioles' infielders screamed at once, "Throw it!"

The second baseman recovered his senses, but it was too late, and all he could do was grit his teeth and check the runner at third.

Gertzy whooped, "Talk about a brain fart!"

They all laughed, Jalen nervously. JY marched out to the plate and caught Jalen's eye. Jalen gave him a thumbs-up, even though he wasn't entirely confident.

Cat gripped Jalen's arm. "This would be a lock for JY to get that new contract. It would be two game-winning moon shots in a row for him. Can you imagine? A grand slam?"

Jalen had the jitters. He twisted free from Cat's hold and croaked, "I know."

36

THE GHOST OF A SMILE CREPT ONTO HARRIS'S
face before he checked it with a frown.

"Slider." Jalen signaled JY with an imaginary throat-cutting motion.

JY blinked, took one more swing, and stepped up to the plate. Harris wound up and let it fly. It started thigh-high toward the middle of the plate. Harris intended that his slider break sharply to the right. JY was ready. He swung and connected.

The ball sailed out of sight, but in the wrong direction, going foul into the stands along the third base line.

Jalen watched the pitcher only for an instant. "Changeup."

He signaled JY, both thumbs up.

The pitch came in low and dropped even lower. JY let it past, and the count was 1–1.

Gertzy slapped Jalen on the back. "Way to go."

Jalen was too intent on Harris to reply. "Oh boy," he said. "This could be it. JY could actually do this. It's gonna be a fastball and he can rip it."

He held up four fingers.

JY saw the signal, and his face relaxed. He was clearly in the zone.

Harris wound up and fired a fastball, chest-high.

JY swung.

The contact of ball and bat made a wonderfully loud, solid sound. The ball soared, high and long. The runners bolted and the crowd sprang to its feet. The center fielder made a mad dash for the wall and took a desperate leap.

37

JALEN WINCED, SHOOK HIS HEAD, AND LOOKED AGAIN.

The center fielder lay like a pile of bones in front of Monument Park in dead center field, 410 feet from home plate. But he held his glove high.

In it was JY's almost grand slam.

Cat gave Jalen's shoulder a squeeze. "You did everything you could do."

"Except help with his first two at bats." Jalen couldn't help feeling glum.

"Yeah, but you told him the pitch, and he almost had it," Gertzy said. "It was awesome."

Even Cat's mom spoke up. "And you know, you can't win them all."

Jalen wanted to let his friends' words sink in and make him feel better, but one look at JY's face ended that.

His nerves were at a high pitch as they waited for JY in the tunnel outside the locker room. Searching for a way to avoid the look he feared was coming, he checked the time on his phone. "Maybe we should get going. We can't be late for practice."

"It's only four twelve," Gertzy said. "We got plenty of time."

"Yeah, but traffic," said Jalen.

"Ha." Gertzy seemed to think Jalen was joking. "You said we were gonna meet JY."

"I'm sure he'll be right out," Cat said.

"Yeah, okay." Jalen was trapped.

They didn't have to wait long. JY came from the locker room in a huff, with his hair soaking wet and a patch of shampoo suds behind one ear. He fumbled to straighten his collar as he stopped to talk. "Foxx wants to see me in his office."

JY gave Cat's mom a worried look.

"It could be good news, James." She gave JY an enthusiastic smile.

"JY, I just have to introduce you to my friend and teammate, Grady Gertz." Jalen pushed Gertzy forward. "Everyone calls him Gertzy."

"Can we take a quick picture, Mr. Yager?" Gertzy's cheeks burned as he handed Jalen his phone.

"Sure, Gertzy." JY posed for the picture and headed for the elevator. He said good-bye over his shoulder and that he'd catch up with them later.

The only one of them who wasn't worried was Gertzy.

In the car, they chatted eagerly, rehashing the game, inning by inning. But the traffic crawled along like thousands of rowboats pushing against some unseen, powerful current, and conversation slowed.

Gertzy looked out his window up at the sky. "If this opens up, we won't even have practice."

"Rain after midnight," Cat said.

"Why are there so many people?" Jalen couldn't help his grumbling. It seemed like the day was as dark as the sky.

"Let's play *Clash*," said Gertzy.

Cat didn't have the game on her phone, but she downloaded it quickly from the app store.

When the traffic cleared and Mrs. H finally sped up, Jalen saw that they were closing in on Bronxville. The middle school where they practiced wasn't far, and they arrived before anyone else was even there.

"It's going to rain cats and dogs," Cat predicted, turning

around to give Jalen a quick wink. It was an old joke between them.

Gertzy assured Cat's mom that they'd be fine. "Even if it does rain, my house is just a five-minute walk, and my mom can take Jalen home."

After good-byes, Jalen and Gertzy hit the locker room, then dumped their gear in the dugout. Jalen took the speed hitter from his bag and stepped outside the dugout to use it. He knew he had to dig deep to make the scouts notice him at the weekend Lakeland tournament. He took a couple of breaths and imagined himself in JY's shoes that afternoon. What made the almost grand slam fall short?

38

INSIDE THE DUGOUT, GERTZY RAISED HIS PHONE.

"You wanna play some more *Clash*?"

Jalen swung and heard the sweet sound of success, like the crack of a bat knocking one out of the park. "Nope. I heard someone say that to master something, you have to do it ten thousand hours."

"Malcolm Gladwell." Gertzy tucked his phone away and took his own speed hitter from his equipment bag.

"What?"

"Not what, who." Gertzy swung nice and easy and the stick popped like a firecracker. "Malcolm Gladwell said that in his book *Outliers*."

"Oh." Jalen swung, but flubbed it. "Shoot."

They both kept swinging, maybe thirty times, most of them good ones. The popping sounds of their sticks echoed off the houses surrounding the school until Fanny arrived and tossed his gear down in the dugout.

After Gunner and Damon arrived, Jalen saw Daniel's dad's big white truck pull into the lot along with a couple of other parents' SUVs.

Gunner and Damon began tossing the ball back and forth, but they were just inside the first base line. Jalen glanced over his shoulder and saw Daniel fast approaching.

"Hey! Ho!" Daniel announced himself as he burst onto the field. "What's the word, my peeps?"

"All right." Coach Allen straightened and blew his whistle. "Everyone in the dugout! Let's go! On me!"

Everyone piled into the dugout. Coach gave his technique speech. Wind whipped up grit from the baselines, stinging their faces, and the dark clouds rolled by overhead. Still, the rain held off.

"Getting ready to squash Lakeland?" Fanny said, clapping his hands, then rubbing them together as if warming them by a fire. "I can't wait to show them our stuff."

Taking a deep breath, Coach said, "We need more to 'squash' Lakeland than 'stuff.'" He looked right at Fanny. "We good? Good. Now, let's get to work."

Gertzy and Jalen tossed the ball back and forth, mixing

in grounders and pop flies as they increased the space between them. Jalen was relieved to see, from the corner of his eye, Daniel warming up with Gunner Petty.

"I'm good. You good?" Gertzy fired a grounder at Jalen.

"We just started." Jalen scooped it up and rifled it back.

"Okay, okay."

Coach blew his whistle to get things going again and the players scrambled. Because rain seemed inevitable, he modified the practice routine and went straight to hitting after warm-ups.

The whistle sounded and they moved on to the directional drill. Gertzy went first. As his partner, Jalen set the balls on the tee. Gertzy tried to hit each of the targets on the backstop: high, low, and middle, and left, right, and center. They each got twenty tries to hit all nine targets in sequential order.

Jalen knew from small talk with other guys on the team that Gertzy typically ripped right through the drill, occasionally going through the whole series twice. After hitting the left-field fly with his first swing, though, Gertzy seemed to lose his composure on the third base line drive. It took him four tries.

Gertzy pounded the grass with his bat and stared at Jalen. "I gotta do better than this if we're gonna beat Lakeland."

To emphasize his point, he jacked his next ball into the middle line drive target.

Gertzy finished the drill with seven of the nine targets under his belt. Jalen struggled. He had been picturing the grand slam with the hitter, like Coach Allen told him. But it didn't make sense to practice making line drives and grounders. He knew he'd heard some MLB superstar say, *I mean, aren't ground balls just another word for outs?* Still, he thought that Coach Allen was a pretty smart guy and Jalen wouldn't waste his time doing something useless. By the time he finished, he'd gotten only five total targets.

The whistle sounded, and they went next to the cage, where Coach Miller pitched to them from behind the L screen. His pitches were perfectly directed.

"Hey! Let's go! You two need a written invitation?" Coach Miller's round face burned red beneath the brim of his Bronxville Bandits cap.

Gertzy held the thick net aside so Jalen could go first. Jalen stepped up to the plate and began bashing hittable, medium-speed pitches.

"Good work." Coach Miller's low growl was high praise, and Jalen bit back a smile as he and Gertzy traded places.

39

"HOW'D IT GO?" DANIEL'S FATHER ASKED AFTER practice.

Daniel chuckled. "Piece of cake. I finally got some extra attention from Coach. Obviously, he sees me as his next star. Lakeland won't know what hit them when me and Jalen get to Tampa."

"Sounds good," Daniel's father said with pleasure in his voice.

In the backseat, Jalen checked his phone.

From Gertzy: Thx for the tix!

Cat wrote: Call 4 news about JY.

Back in Rockton, Jalen hopped out in front of his house and said good-bye. The sun was nearly down, and the shadows were deep. He dialed up Cat before Daniel's dad was out of sight.

"Why didn't you just text me what's going on?" Jalen complained as soon as Cat answered.

"Some things you just don't put into writing," said Cat.

"Why?"

Cat paused before saying, "I don't know why. They always say that in action films."

"Okay. . . . So what's the big deal?"

"JY is getting traded to Atlanta."

Jalen dropped his gear and paced up and down in the driveway as he spoke. "But Foxx said he'd sign JY to a new contract if he batted a thousand! He said it to everyone! It's online! It's in the news!"

Cat huffed. "I know. We both know. We said that. Now Foxx says the direction of the team is changing. They need to, quote, get younger to stay competitive. Blah, blah. They brought up a utility infielder from AAA so Reuben Hall can get more reps at second. And Reuben Hall is just as good as JY, only with more upside. He had all the numbers."

"What numbers?" Jalen yelled.

"You? The baseball genius?" Cat teased. "'What numbers?'"

"I wasn't thinking straight," Jalen said.

Cat continued, "Foxx already said on the news that if it

were up to him he'd keep JY, but times are changing, and he has to think about the good of the team. Can you believe that garbage? The advanced stats say dump JY and get younger, so that's what they do, follow the analytics. Don't think about what you see JY do on the field. . . . Of course, Foxx thinks JY stinks without you."

Cat waited for Jalen to respond, but he didn't.

"You have nothing to say," she taunted.

Jalen exploded. "That rat. That skunk! I can't stand when someone like Foxx wins." He removed his cap and ran his fingers through his hair. "What's going to happen to my dad . . . and the Silver Liner franchise?"

"But your dad already signed the deal, right?" Cat's voice brightened.

"Yeah, but what if it all falls apart? If JY stops tweeting—if he stops playing—do people stop going? Does it all disappear, like a dream?"

"No," Cat said. "No."

"Then why'd you say it twice?" Jalen asked.

"What?"

"No. You said no twice."

Cat hesitated. "Did I? Well, I didn't mean anything by it. Or I meant, 'No, the Silver Liner restaurant chain won't go away,' and 'No, nothing bad is going to happen to your dad.'"

Jalen realized he'd been shouting when the porch lights popped on. The door opened and his dad peered into the gloom. "Jalen? Is that you?"

"Gotta go, Cat." Jalen disconnected and grabbed his bag. "Yeah, Dad, it's me. What are you doing home?"

40

JALEN'S DAD STEPPED OUT ONTO THE PORCH AND
opened his arms wide. "I surprise you, no?"

"Yes." Jalen's mind spun with possibilities as he climbed
the steps. "Is everything okay?"

"Why you ask me that? 'Cause I not cooking tonight at
the restaurant, right?" His dad reached for Jalen's equipment bag. "Let me help you."

Jalen let go of the bag and followed his dad inside.
The smell of sauce cooking tickled his nose. "Well, yeah.
You're never home this early. Is the Silver Liner okay? Is
the franchise deal still on?"

His dad hung the bag and motioned Jalen toward the
kitchen. "Oh, you talking about Mr. JY getting the trade?

That's not gonna hurt the franchise. They already telling me Atlanta is just another moneymaking place for the Silver Liner. That man you met at the diner—I call him the chief. He says Atlanta is gonna love my cooking."

"Dad, that's great."

"Yes, yes. You sit. I got *nonna*'s chicken cacciatore over homemade linguini. You like, no?"

"I love." Jalen sat down.

"You love! That's the music to my ears." His dad dipped a wooden spoon into the steaming pot on the stove. He smacked his lips and added a pinch of salt.

Jalen filled a glass with milk from a carton on the table but paused before drinking. "So, what's up? Why the special dinner?"

His dad came over and sat across from him, still smiling. "First thing tomorrow I fly to Atlanta. I'm gonna be gone for a few days to see the new place we gonna have a Silver Liner Diner. And I tell them if I gotta go, I gotta take a night to see my boy."

His dad frowned. "They want me to travel? Is okay, I can travel, but anytime I take the trip, I also gotta have the time off to see my boy. So, tonight we gonna eat and then we gonna watch a movie on that new big screen. Just you an' me."

Jalen returned his dad's beaming smile. "Thanks, Dad. What are we gonna watch?"

"What you wanna watch?"

Jalen shrugged. "Cat always tells me I gotta see *Avengers: Infinity War* sometime, so maybe that?"

"Is *Avengers*, then." His dad slapped his leg and returned to cooking their dinner. From the stove, he said, "I gonna call Daniel's father to see if maybe you stay there for while I'm gone. Then you go with the team to Tampa and I get you from the airport to come home."

"Uh, okay."

"What? Is Daniel's house no good?" his dad asked.

"It's okay, but maybe I could stay with Cat. Daniel already shares a room with his sister, so things are kinda tight." It was true, but Jalen had another reason. Mrs. H already knew about his mom, so it'd be easier to see her if he stayed at Mount Tipton.

"You think is okay even though she's a girl?" His dad turned toward him with raised eyebrows.

"Dad."

His dad threw his hands in the air. "Okay, okay, I don't know how all this boy-and-girl thing works today. Back in Italy, a father don't need to ask. The girl's papa lets the boy's papa know. I don't know if she's the girlfriend or the friend, so I gotta ask."

Jalen shook his head wildly. "No, no, no. Not girlfriend. No girlfriend. Just friend. Best friend, even, but not girlfriend."

"Okay, I hear you. So, I'm gonna call who?" His dad dumped the boiling pasta into a strainer in the sink.

"Cat's mom," Jalen said.

His dad shook the strainer. Steam clouded his glasses. He brought a heaping platter to the table and declared, "First we eat, then I'm gonna call the mom, then we watching the movie."

Jalen took a big bite. "The cacciatore is delicious, Dad. It always is."

Jalen tore a piece of bread from the loaf on the table, dipped it in *nonna*'s tangy sauce, and said, "How are you doing with the chefs?"

"They want to learn, Jalen. They want to know what Fabio knows. What *nonna* taught Fabio."

After the fabulous dinner, Jalen's dad brought out his melt-in-your mouth tiramisu. It even looked delicious, with cocoa sprinkled on top of the custard and ladyfingers, just the way his father had learned in Italy.

After gobbling down the rich dessert, Jalen was surprised when his dad said, "I never tell you about your mother. Maybe that was a big mistake . . . maybe I should have told you. I can only say I was never a father before, and I had nobody to get the advice."

Jalen listened intently.

"We were happy together. So happy when you were

born. But she couldn't stop singing. Some agent comes along and tells her she's going to be a big star. She can't give up opportunity of a lifetime. So she flies away. Your mom, she's like a butterfly. She had to go. She said you'd be better off with me. She knew I'd never leave you."

Jalen's eyes grew wider. Here was the story he'd been waiting for. "But you said she only married you so you could get your green card."

"I didn't wanna to hurt you. I don't know what to say, so I say that."

"Why tell me now?" Jalen asked.

Did his dad know she was back?

"I gotta know you growing up. Almost a man. I think, my boy needs to know."

Emotion flooded Jalen. He pushed back his chair.

His father stood at the same time, and they embraced, sharing feelings without words, before pulling away.

"What about that TV?" Jalen said.

Jalen's dad fell asleep before the Hulk crash-landed in the Sanctum Sanctorum.

Eye-popping as the movie was, Jalen couldn't really enjoy it. He decided to pause it, took his phone with him into the bathroom, and dialed his mom. She answered right away.

"Mom, I'm sorry it took me so long."

"Oh, Jalen. Don't think about it. I felt bad about interrupting you."

Jalen kept his voice low. "It was just a bad situation. I was trying to help JY, and it kind of didn't work."

"We saw," said his mom. "George told me about the trade to Atlanta. I'm sure you're upset about that."

"Well, Dad thinks it'll be okay. Just another place for a Silver Liner." Jalen put the cover down and sat on the toilet. "I haven't even spoken to JY."

"I've got about fifteen minutes before my second set."

"Sorry, I forgot you're singing tonight, Mom."

"No more sorrys, Jalen," she said gently. "We're not strangers talking to each other, are we? We're family." She paused to let that sink in. "What do you think about George's idea? The direct approach, where the three of us just walk right into the restaurant and sit down to talk?"

"Mom, I need a little more time to find the right approach."

"But Jalen, you don't have to put all this on yourself. George and I think it's not as . . . big a problem as you think it is."

"But . . . but I don't know where to start."

"See, that's just it," she said. "You don't have to.

"We will!"

41

"NO, NO, NO, NO." JALEN JUMPED TO HIS FEET. "YOU
and George can't just . . . go right at him, guns blazing."

"No, not like that at all!" his mother said reassuringly.
"We don't want to shock Fabio. Or hurt him—but talk honestly and directly and let him know that, like George said
to me, we're not looking for him to trade you to our team.
Just that we'd like to join the team you and he already
have."

They both fell silent as Jalen's mom let him think it
through.

It was an exciting possibility, one team.

"I don't know how Dad's gonna like being on any team
that George is on. No offense."

"Jalen, your father is a grown-up!" His mom took a breath and her voice softened. "It's been a long time. People change . . . and grow."

Jalen stood up and found himself looking in the mirror. "It's just the way he looks at your picture."

"My picture?"

"It's . . . in my room." Jalen's cheeks burned even though no one could see him. "It's an old picture of you smiling. It's in a frame on my bookshelf. I look at it kind of a lot. Dad, not so much. But whenever he does pick it up? He gets this look on his face. Like he's wishing. He said you two were happy." Jalen heard the pleading in his voice. "Were you happy?" In the mirror he saw both his mom's and dad's features in his own face.

"We were good together for a while, your dad and me. Why shouldn't he remember that time fondly? I think I was in love with love."

"What does that even mean?" Jalen demanded.

After a pause, his mom said, "Jalen, it's not always easy to explain what happens with people. I was in love and then I wanted more. Your father understood."

"He said you were like a butterfly."

"He let me go. Jalen, I believe things happen for a reason, even though we sometimes don't understand. You have to have faith, and you have to have hope. This is a delicate situation, but it's not an impossible situation. As long as we're honest and kind, things will work out. I promise."

"'Honest and kind,' that's like something my dad would say." Jalen sighed. "Okay, I get it. I'd like it better if you could tell him. Just you, Mom. Not George. Okay?"

She was silent for a moment before she said, "Jalen, I think George should be there."

Alarm flooded Jalen's veins. "But you told me you'd do whatever I want."

"No, not whatever you want."

"What?"

"Yes. Your father needs to know up front that George is part of the package," Jalen's mom said firmly. "He needs to see that so there can't be any misunderstanding. You see that's true, don't you, dear?"

Jalen closed his eyes and tried to wrap his mind around it. Finally he said, "Well, Dad's leaving first thing tomorrow, so you won't be able to see him until the weekend. I'll be gone until Monday night, so that'll at least give him some time to settle down."

"You think he's going to be so upset?" she asked.

"I don't know. I just said it like that. I didn't mean anything one way or the other."

"Where are you going this weekend?" she asked.

"To the Lakeland tournament near Tampa. It's big-time,

Mom, and we only got asked because we won the tournament in Boston."

"Fantastic! Congratulations, Jalen." Her voice rose with excitement. "Maybe we can come cheer you on?"

"Uh, sure."

"Would you rather we didn't? We certainly don't have to." She sounded nice about it but was obviously disappointed.

Jalen paused. He wanted her to stay around so she could talk to his dad, but he also liked the idea of having her there rooting him on. "No, that's okay. I'd like it if you were there."

"And George, too?"

"Sure. George, too." He remembered the plan. "I'm gonna be staying with Cat while Dad's gone, so maybe you can come over. I think you'd really like Cat's mom. She's great."

"That sounds brilliant. But we can't let this go on indefinitely, Jalen. It *will* hurt Fabio to know that you were afraid to tell him."

"I know, I know," Jalen agreed reluctantly. "So I'll check with Cat and let you know, but I'm sure it'll be fine."

"George is signaling me. I've got to go—"

"Thanks, Mom."

"I didn't do anything."

"Well, have a great show." Jalen said good-bye and returned to the movie. With his mind on other things, he watched to the end before waking his dad.

"Is over?" his father asked after looking around and blinking.

Jalen helped him out of the chair. "It's late, Dad. Let's go to sleep."

"Okay," said his dad. "We have fun, no?"

"Yeah, Dad. Dinner was great. The movie, too."

When Jalen got into bed, his father bent to rest his hand on his cheek. "You make all this happen for us, Jalen. You know this?"

Jalen grabbed his dad's hand with both of his, and he kissed the rough skin on the knuckles. "I love you, Dad. More than anything."

"I love you, too, Jalen. You the best boy in the whole world."

Jalen's smile melted away as his dad disappeared, shutting the door behind him.

Would his father think he was so great when he learned what Jalen had done? He tossed and turned. He felt like his long-lost mother was prodding him to turn his father's world upside down. To wreck his dad's happiness just when things were going so well. How could he?

The more the time on the clock chewed away at the night, the less Jalen thought of himself.

The big red numbers on the clock said 12:14 when the first rumble of thunder shook the house. Soon it sounded like a fireworks display. Lightning cracked and flashed so bright outside the window that Jalen jumped out of bed to pull the curtains shut before jumping right back in beneath his covers.

Then came the rain. Spouts of wind-whipped water thrashed the roof. The noise and the mayhem matched the confusion in Jalen's brain.

Finally the rain eased into a steady thrumming, the thunder faded to a ghostly echo, and Jalen drifted off to sleep.

42

HE WOKE TO A BRILLIANT BAND OF SUNSHINE
that had shouldered its way into the bedroom between
the curtains. He jumped up, but his dad was long gone.
He'd left a handwritten note on the kitchen table wishing
Jalen luck and saying he couldn't wait to pick him up at
the airport Monday night.

Jalen packed a bag for Cat's and a second for the tournament at Lakeland. He poured some Raisin Bran into a
bowl and ate hurriedly. Cat and her mom were coming
to pick him up in an hour. Jalen used the time to do reps
with his speed hitter in the front yard.

The Range Rover pulled up, and Jalen loaded his bags
and his gear in back. He climbed into the backseat and

wasted no time bringing up the subject of his mom.

"So I thought I should invite my mom over to your house. Is that okay, Mrs. H?"

"Cat and I wanted to spend the afternoon by the pool anyway." Cat's mom glanced at him in the mirror. "I think James is going to stop by to say good-bye. Your mom is more than welcome to join us. I'll have some sandwiches made up."

"What about her—" Jalen just did not want to say "boyfriend." "What about George?"

"Of course he's welcome."

"You're the best, Mrs. Hewlett." He texted his mom.

He read her reply and proudly said, "Mom wants to know what she can bring."

Cat spun around with her face lit up. "How about some Scribblers? You know, those ice pops that look like big crayons?"

"Tell her that's very nice of her, but just bring themselves," Cat's mom said. "You don't need more sugar, Catrina."

"Who's Catrina?" Cat asked.

Her mom rolled her eyes.

"You are what you eat, Mom." Cat fished a Jolly Rancher out of her pocket and popped it into her mouth. "And you know I'm sweet."

Jalen knew enough to stay quiet, but he texted his mom and asked her to bring Scribblers anyway. He assumed George would be impressed to meet JY. He quickly gave himself a mental kick in the butt, because who cared about impressing George?

"I'm surprised JY's still here," Jalen said, thinking out loud. "I think Atlanta plays the Phillies tomorrow night. Albies is out with a broken thumb, and I think the guy they brought up from Gwinnett is struggling on offense."

Cat's mom said, "I didn't know you followed the Braves."

"Mom," Cat said. "He's a genius, remember? He glances at the box scores and shazam!—he can tell you anything on the page, even from, like, fifty years ago."

"Not from fifty years." Jalen knew he was blushing.

"Only because you haven't looked at numbers from fifty years ago. Am I right?" Cat asked.

Jalen shrugged.

"Anyway," Cat's mom said. "They did tell him they want him for tomorrow's game. He's got a two thirty-five flight to Atlanta. That's why I said I *think* he's stopping by. He might not have time."

Jalen wasn't sure he wanted to see the ex-Yankee. He knew JY wanted to finish his career as a lifelong Yankee, like Derek Jeter and Mariano Rivera. Then he realized something important. JY didn't have to be traded.

According to the contract the ownership had with all the players, he'd been on one team so long that he couldn't be forced into a trade. He had to accept the trade. Maybe JY saw Atlanta as a new beginning.

Maybe he wouldn't blame Jalen.

43

THEY PASSED THROUGH THE BIG IRON GATES AND
the ten-foot stone walls of Mount Tipton, up the long, curving drive among the fat twisted trees, past the stables, and arrived at the garages in the back. A young man in black pants and matching polo shirt whisked away Jalen's bags without a word.

The massive stone house was practically ancient, but the pool was pretty new. At least eight people could sit comfortably in the giant hot tub. The furniture cushions, umbrellas, and fluffy beach towels all had blue-and-white stripes. After all the rain, it was a beautiful day. Sunlight warmed the ground and winked in the ripples of the pool made by the breeze.

"I'm going to change into a swimsuit," Mrs. H said. "Jalen, make yourself comfortable. Cat?"

"My suit's on." Cat lifted her shirt and showed off a blaze of yellow.

Her mom frowned. "Cat, a lady changes into her swimsuit."

Cat shrugged. "Good thing I'm still a girl, huh?"

"All right, miss. Don't get too high on your horse." Mrs. H turned to go. "I'll be back."

Cat slumped down in a lounge chair under some shade. "Sorry my mom is such a grouch."

Jalen sat in a swivel chair beside her so he could rock. "She's not."

Cat tilted her head at him. "Yeah. She is. But I think it's because JY is going, and there's nothing we can do about that. We tried, right?"

Jalen looked at the laces of his sneakers, red to match the Bronxville Bandits colors. "I thought you didn't want to talk about JY and your mom."

"I don't." Cat scowled. "But it's in my face. I can run, but I can't hide."

"So, what do you think is going on?" Jalen thought he knew, and it struck a chord of fear deep in his heart.

Cat put on a pair of sunglasses and turned her head toward the pool and the rolling green wooded hills beyond.

"Last time she looked at someone like this, it was my step-father, before he took her to the south of France in his private jet. After that, the only thing left was the paperwork for the lawyers."

Jalen sighed. "Aren't you sick of grown-ups acting like kids?"

Cat turned her head toward him. "You won't find me getting married three or four times, I can tell you."

"You think she's gonna marry JY?" That, Jalen realized, was what scared him. That Cat would move away to Atlanta.

"I really don't know," Cat said. "But I'm sure it's on the table. My stepfather isn't even around. The first couple of months we came to Tipton they were so in love, you needed a crowbar to pry them apart. Now he spends most of his time in China."

The arrival of Jalen's mom and George, led by the same young man who had taken Jalen's luggage, brought an unsettled end to their discussion.

Jalen jumped out of his seat and shook hands with George. He and his mom gave each other a big hug. Cat shook their hands and offered them chairs. His mom produced a plastic grocery bag with a box of Scribblers. "For you and Jalen," she said.

"Oh, thank you." Cat peered into the bag and dug out two pops, giving them to Jalen.

"You're very welcome."

"Don't eat mine while I put the rest of them in the freezer," Cat teased before leaving.

Jalen and his mom and George settled into the big lounge chairs, an awkward silence between them. He was relieved when Cat returned with her mom, who appeared in a robe and swimsuit that matched her dark hair, partly hidden by a wide-brimmed sun hat.

Smiling at Jalen's mom, Mrs. H said, "I remember you from the championship game last Sunday." She introduced herself to George as Cat's mom, Tory, her smile welcoming them both.

George immediately started talking about "what a smashing country pile" Mrs. H had. Jalen expected her to get angry—he would have if George called his house a pile—but Mrs. H lapped it up like a kitten with a dish of milk.

As Mrs. H and Jalen's mom got talking, George took something from under his arm and placed it on the ground beside his chair. It appeared to be some kind of winter glove—orange and blue and black, folded in half, only with a web between the thumb and first finger.

George saw Jalen looking, and he raised the foreign-looking glove in his hand. "Wicketkeeper."

"What?"

George put it under his arm and gave Jalen a salute. "From my schoolboy days at Harrow. Before my growth spurt, I was rather short and played wicketkeeper on the cricket pitch. I thought maybe you and I could have a catch later on. With a baseball, of course. Not a cricket ball. That would be like playing catch with rocks," he said jovially.

"Oh." Jalen stared at the brightly colored glove. "Sure." He couldn't tell if George was making fun of him or just having a good time.

Mrs. H was sharing a laugh with Jalen's mom.

The adults made small talk while several waiters set up a serving table and loaded it with sandwiches, salads, and a wooden bowl filled with individual bags of chips.

They chatted on and on about London and New York and the differences as well as the similarities of their two favorite cities. Cat pulled her chair partially into the sun and lay back as if she hadn't a care in the world. Jalen sat rigidly upright, wearing his mirror sunglasses. His shaded eyes—but not his ears—followed the conversation. He was surprised to hear his name and realize they were all looking at him.

44

"SORRY." JALEN SNAPPED TO WITH BURNING CHEEKS.

His mother said, "George asked how you think your team will do this weekend."

"Oh. Sorry. The tournament is with the top sixteen teams in the country, so I don't know."

"That sounds exciting." George looked at Jalen's mom. "I'm with you. We should go."

"But aren't you singing?" Jalen asked.

"New talent comes in for the weekend," George said.

"What George politely said is that I'm not a headliner."

"Not yet," George put in.

"I'm not a headliner yet, so I only play midweek in bigger clubs."

"Worse luck for the patrons, my dear, because there is no singer working today as fine as you."

"Well, that's lucky for me," Jalen said, thinking of the game.

"You sure you want us?" Jalen's mom asked.

"Yes, I'm sure," he said.

His mom looked at George. "Let's."

George pulled out his phone. "I'll get our tickets. When is your first game?"

"Friday at five o'clock."

George nodded.

"Cat?" Mrs. H asked. "Want to take a trip to Tampa?"

Cat sat up and removed her sunglasses. "Coach Allen said I could keep stats, you know. I didn't in Boston because I was busy with JY, but he's not holding that against me. He's some change from Coach Gamble. Right, Jalen?"

Everyone turned toward Jalen. "Right. He's great."

Mrs. H took her phone from her robe pocket. "Tampa it is. What flights do you have, George? We may as well go down together."

They booked their flights and Mrs. H suggested lunch.

Jalen was biting into a roast beef sandwich when JY appeared. The baseball legend wore aviator sunglasses, and his hair was gelled back. His face had the shadow of a beard. Jalen caught a whiff of some pleasant-smelling cologne.

He jumped up and shook JY's hand. Cat's mom took ahold of JY's arm and introduced him to George as James Yager. He shook hands, said to call him JY, and gave Jalen's mom a kiss on the cheek.

"There's lunch," Cat's mom said.

"Thanks. I ate." JY sat down next to Jalen in the shade and looked at his watch. "I only have a few minutes, but I wanted to say good-bye. And show you the start of the beard I've always wanted to grow."

Jalen nodded, remembering that all Yankees had to be clean-shaven.

"I don't know if Jalen told you, but I'm a big fan," George said.

JY gave Jalen's shoulder a friendly squeeze and nodded at the glove under George's chair. "He didn't. Cricket, right?"

George lifted the glove. "Wicketkeeper. Right. The father of your baseball."

JY chuckled. "Abner Doubleday is the father of baseball."

George shook his head, exposing big, crooked teeth with his smile. "If you dig into your history, there are accounts of 'base ball' being played in England in the 1750s. America and England were still playing cricket matches back then."

"I suppose next you'll tell me the Americans didn't take Normandy in World War II." JY was still chuckling.

"You Yanks did a bang-up job on *your* two beaches, as we did on ours. But I'm sure you haven't forgotten how long we Brits fought that terrible war before you joined in." George's face was dead serious.

"Well, our two countries have a special relationship, don't we?" JY's smile looked as if it was pasted on. "How would you like me to sign your glove?"

JY reached for it, but George pulled it back. "Thank you, but it's already signed by Mark Boucher, the South African. Nine hundred and ninety-nine dismissals? No? Well, cricket's not everyone's game, is it?" he said with a broad grin.

Jalen wanted to crawl under a rock.

"Wait!" Cat said abruptly, offering a most welcome change of subject.

"I'm sorry," she said softly. "I didn't mean to startle everyone, but George, maybe you should get JY to sign your baseball?"

George looked confused. Cat nodded at the glove.

George's face brightened and he unfolded the glove, revealing a brand-new baseball that he offered up to JY. "Quite right. That would be smashing."

"And smashing is a good thing?" JY asked.

"Yes, a brilliant thing."

"I guess you could say that smashing a baseball is smashing."

Both men laughed as JY autographed the baseball.

"So, we've come full circle." JY turned his smile on Jalen. "The day I met you, you were stealing autographed baseballs, and the day we say good-bye, I'm autographing a baseball for free."

"I—" Jalen choked on his words.

JY laughed and everyone joined in except Jalen, who was too flustered to do anything but sputter. He wanted to explain to his mom and George that he'd taken the balls only because there were so many of them lying around JY's batting cage, and he only took the few he needed to pay the fee for his travel baseball team.

"Don't worry." JY thumped Jalen on the back as he stood. "I appreciate what you've done for me. My lucky charm. Even though the Yankees and I decided on an ami-cable divorce." He seemed to wink at Mrs. H, but Jalen couldn't swear to it. "You and your friends—hey, where's Mr. Hot Sauce?"

Jalen and Cat looked at each other, and Jalen said, "I think he's working with his dad."

At the same time, Cat said, "Watching his sister."

"Well, you guys helped me out when I thought I needed

some help. Now, on to the greener pastures of Georgia. A fresh start. Anytime you need Braves tickets . . ." JY bumped fists with everyone all around before giving Cat's mom a big hug.

"I'm rotten at good-byes," JY said, turning away.

"I'll walk you to your car," Cat's mom said.

They were walking toward the driveway when JY looked back and shouted, "Hey, Jalen! If it works out with your schedule, maybe you'll come down to Atlanta sometime and call a few pitches! You can bring your friends! On me!"

Jalen cupped his hands around his mouth. "You got it, JY!"

"Just call his agent!" shouted Cat.

As they disappeared down the path, JY's laughter bubbled up into the trees, only to be lost in the whisper of their abundant leaves.

"Wow," Jalen said, after a minute of silence. "That happened so fast."

"Most pro ballplayers move around," said Cat.

"He was such a big part of the Yankees," Jalen said.

"Only not Jeffrey Foxx's Yankees," Cat said.

"Foxx is a rat." Jalen opened a bag of chips. "Still, JY is a lot less broken up about it than I would have thought."

Cat's mom came back wearing a dark pair of sunglasses. As they finished eating, George asked Jalen, "How about a catch?"

In an easy voice, Jalen's mom asked, "Is there somewhere I can change into my swimsuit?"

"Let me show you." Mrs. H led the way to the cabana. George removed his blazer and rolled up his sleeves. Jalen walked over to a flat patch of grass.

"So, what we do in baseball when we have a catch is make it hard on each other, ugly ground balls, pop flies, line drives." Jalen didn't plan on making it easy for the old man. "You field it, then you zip it to the other guy. He zips it back, and then you switch."

"And what's a zip?" George asked, rolling his sleeves even tighter.

"You know, you put some heat on it. Some hot sauce." Jalen paused. "You throw it hard and fast. Here, toss me the ball and I'll show you."

"Brilliant." George tossed the ball underhand.

"Ready?" asked Jalen as he tossed the ball up and caught it, trying not to smirk at George's innocent smile.

Jalen rifled the ball at George.

He snapped it up and zipped it back in one easy motion. The ball popped when it hit the meaty part of Jalen's hand. It stung.

"Nice. Ready?" Jalen reared back and fired a nasty grounder that took a double hop.

George snatched it and threw it back like a pro. This time Jalen was careful to catch the ball in the webbing of his glove.

When it was Jalen's turn, George sent the ball flying skyward so that it shrank to a speck before dropping twenty feet to Jalen's left. He didn't get exactly under it and had to dive in the grass to save it.

"Blinding!" shouted George. "A most excellent save."

"I play second base," Jalen said, firing the ball back to George, "so I don't see pop flies like that."

"It was well-played, nonetheless." George returned the ball and braced his hands on his bent knees, apparently ready for anything.

They played for a good half hour before Jalen ran inside to retrieve his speed hitter and show George. Jalen gave him a demonstration that sounded like a gun range, snapping the stick and making it look easy before giving George a try.

"Now, you know in cricket we use a paddle and we hold it like this." George turned the stick so it pointed straight down. "A cricket bowler, unlike a baseball pitcher, is required to bounce the ball before it reaches the batter." He swung up, like a baseball swing turned ninety degrees.

"How do you hit it like that?" Jalen asked.

"The same way you hit it like this." George brought the stick back over his shoulder like a baseball player and swung for the stars.

Nothing.

Jalen reached for the stick. "You—"

"Wait, wait, wait!" George pulled the stick out of Jalen's reach and took a giant swing.

Nothing.

He swung again.

Nothing.

Again.

Nada.

The frustrated look on George's face was too much for Jalen, and he burst out laughing.

George raised the stick over his head like a club.

Jalen kept laughing.

45

THE STICK CAME DOWN IN AN ARC.

Like a pendulum, it kept going through the bottom of the arc and came back up and through, like finishing a golf swing.

POP!

"Well, you got it that way. Is that the way you swing a cricket paddle?"

"Bat," George replied. "It's a cricket bat." He studied the stick intently. "So, it's in the wrists, is it?"

"And the speed. You need both." Because Jalen felt bad about laughing at George, he decided to share his secret. "What I do is I visualize my swing, every time, right before I take it."

Jalen took the stick and stood in his batter's stance. He gazed at the distant hills between the trees. "What I'm seeing is myself swinging and hitting the biggest prize in the game."

Jalen swung and the stick popped.

"A home run," said George.

"Nope." Jalen handed back the stick. "Bigger, a game-winning grand slam."

"Grand slam. Quite right. Gives your mates four rib eye steaks with one mighty blow."

Jalen looked at George, wondering again if he was making fun or simply knew a lot more than he let on.

"Four rib eyes in one swing. You got it exactly."

George tried a few more times before giving up the stick to Jalen. Jalen hit twenty more imaginary grand slams and then shut it down so he could spend some time with his mom. He'd never been much for sitting in the sun, but there she lay, right next to Cat and her mom, soaking it in. Jalen took the lounge chair next to his mom and adjusted it so he was mostly in the shade. George sat down, also in the shade, with his phone.

Jalen's mom raised up on her elbows. "You two looked like you were having fun."

George looked up. "I have a new appreciation for grand-slam home runs."

"You've got a great glove, even if it isn't made of leather. That's for sure."

"Actually, it is leather and composite. I suppose the flash colors are off-putting."

"*That's* for sure," Jalen said, and slouched back in his chair.

His mom reached out and took hold of his hand. He looked around, embarrassed, until he realized no one was paying attention, not even George.

He gave her hand a squeeze. "Mom, I've been meaning to tell you that I was sorry to hear about your mom and dad, you know, dying in a car crash."

She squeezed his fingers tight, sat up, and removed her sunglasses. He thought she might cry, but instead she took a deep breath through her nose and cleared her throat. "Thank you."

She fell silent and sat back. He wished he could hear what she was thinking.

"We lost touch over the years. That made it even worse. You always think there'll be time to say everything you need to say. Then you get a phone call in the middle of the night."

Jalen felt bad that he'd brought it up. "That's how Emery found you. Their names were on your wedding license and the accident was in the paper."

She smiled and shook her head. "My father gave me a toy doctor's kit when I was around eight. It was the only gift I ever got outside Christmas or my birthday. I got straight As in high school and they began to call me Dr. Johnson at home, but the church choir director—heck, the whole congregation—said I had genuine musical talent."

She looked out over the wooded hills and spoke in barely a whisper. "My grandmother was so cold. She was just relentlessly angry that her brother had been killed by Italian soldiers in World War II. And because she lived with my folks, it was very ugly. It's hard to believe she could be so bitter after so long."

George came over and spoke bluffly. "Nonsense, Lizzie, my dear! Time is like a mountain river at flood. An ancestor of mine was cheated out of a rather ripping country house in 1684. Cheated at cards, don'tcha know! . . . Well, the upshot is that we don't acknowledge the cheater's descendants to this very day. Family cuts them dead at court do's."

Cat's mom perked up. "Court? Do you mean the queen's court?"

"Yes, Tory, he does. My George is actually Lord—"Jalen's mom began.

George cut her off by touching her lips ever so slightly.

"Elizabeth, I don't use a title at home, so I most certainly won't use it here. I'm just plain old doddering George."

Jalen wasn't even taken aback by George's speech. He was determined to say what he felt.

"I'm sorry," he said, talking directly to his mom. "I shouldn't have brought it up. I hurt you."

She held up her hand to stop him. "No, of course you didn't. You have every right to, anyway. And then there's me."

She bit her lip, and her body tightened. "I've been gone most of your life, and you had to use your 'genius' money to find me. Now here I am, with no invitation and no right to break into your life, hoping to be welcomed."

"I'm glad you're here," Jalen said. "Welcome to my life."

She choked back a sound, half a sob and half a laugh.

Jalen realized they'd stopped holding hands. He sat up and turned to face her on his lounge chair to see her better. "Do you ever regret not becoming a doctor?"

She thought deeply before locking on his eyes. "Five years ago, I released a single: 'Steel Whisper.' It went to number one in Amsterdam in a week, and boy, we knew it was gonna catch fire in Europe, Athens, Rome, Berlin, then Paris and London. After that, George just knew we'd sign a big deal with an American label. I was gonna be as big as Adele. We celebrated for three days like we'd won a five-hundred-million-dollar Powerball."

She sighed and fell silent.

Jalen waited, then asked, "So what happened?"

46

"YOU WERE PROBABLY TOO YOUNG TO REMEMBER, but the economy took a hit. The clubs were empty. My record took a nosedive. But for three days, I was a star, and everyone around me believed it as well because I believed it."

After a pause, Jalen asked, "Are you saying it was all worth it?"

She fell silent. The wind bent the trees. Jalen realized he had dug his nails into his palms.

"Yes," she said. "I still believe I can do it. I'm at the Jazz Forum in Tarrytown. That's a big start toward cracking New York. I don't know if this is what you want, but . . . I am sorry."

Jalen shrugged. "Plenty of kids have just a dad or just a mom, and none are better than my dad. I just wanted to know you, and have you know me."

She picked up his hand in both of hers and kissed it. "I want that too. I really do."

Jalen let his head fall back.

He relaxed, listening to the sounds of an early summer afternoon in the country, until she sighed and said, "You know, I really can't wait to see Fabio."

Jalen's mom and George skipped out before dinner, much to the disappointment of Mrs. H. They had an appointment to entertain a club owner from Chicago. That left more steak and fixin's for Jalen and Cat.

After dinner, they discussed the finer points of *Clash Royale* strategy while Mrs. H read and listened to a demo CD that Jalen's mom had given her as a visiting gift. Jalen was totally impressed by his mother's sultry voice. He had never heard jazz singing before, but he also had never heard his mother singing before. It was nearly impossible to concentrate on *Clash Royale*, and he went to sleep hearing the lyrics to "Someone to Watch Over Me" like an ear worm he didn't want to shake out.

He felt really great the next morning. After a big breakfast, he packed for the practice Coach Allen had scheduled but got an unexpected text.

Practice canceled. Coach Miller and I have unexpected commitments. See you all @ airport tomorrow.

Well, if Daniel was free, they could do some drills. But first, it was a great day for Cat and him to do some extra work.

Around lunchtime, his phone rang. It was a number he didn't recognize, and who called these days?

"Jalen, I'm thrilled to get you," George said cheerily. "Your mother and I have a little proposition for you. Since you and your friends and Mrs. Hewlett have all been so hospitable, Lizzie and I wondered if we could reciprocate."

"Sure," Jalen said. "How?"

"We thought you might enjoy hearing your mother's closing-night set at the club tonight, in Tarrytown."

Jalen had no need to think. "I want to go. You bet!"

"And the others?"

"My guess is yes. Mrs. H loved Mom's CD," Jalen said. "Me too."

So that evening, aided by a maps app, Cat guided her mother to the other side of the county, the Hudson River side. They parked in a bank parking lot and made their way to a modest little building with a small sign that read JAZZ FORUM ARTS. Jalen couldn't help feeling that it was pretty unimpressive compared with Yankee Stadium, but Mrs. H immediately said, "How charming. And how *exciting*. Cat,

I haven't been to a jazz club since long before I met your father."

They were greeted inside by the owner, Mark, who made a big thing out of seating them personally after he knew who they were. The room was packed tight with small tables and chairs, and Mark led them to a RESERVED table near the stage. Jalen thought it must be the stage, even though it was at the same level as the tables, because there was a piano grouped with chairs and music stands.

George came out and said they should order anything they liked, on his tab. Beaming, he added, "Nothing is too good for the artist's son."

"Is my mom here?" Jalen asked hesitantly.

"Of course she is. But Lizzie, like all great artists, is cloistered away, concentrating on her performance to come."

"I get it. It's like starting pitchers who don't want to talk to anyone on game day."

"Sounds unsociable. All day?"

"Absolutely, George," Cat piped up. "Some guys don't want anybody to talk with them before the game or during the game—and maybe even after the game if they pitch badly."

After replying that he could appreciate that, George excused himself. As the club filled up and the noise level grew, Jalen, Cat, and Mrs. H picked at their plates and chatted a little more. It was a shock when Mark picked up a microphone and asked for quiet during the upcoming performance.

"Huh! Try that at a Yankees game," Cat quipped.

Then he asked for all cell phones to be turned off, and the show began.

The next hour was a blur to Jalen. Too much happened that was new to him. His mother took words and wrapped them around him like a warm, fuzzy blanket. Even when she sang fast songs or sang with just sounds—not words at all—it was aimed at him, just like her eyes were locked in on him.

All he could remember for certain was that his mom's last song was like an old friend: "Someone to Watch Over Me."

It was an amazing, incredible night. It was as warm and reassuring as his father's food, as satisfying as calling pitches right for JY . . . as great as—he didn't know what.

When the applause died down a little, his mom stopped throwing kisses to the audience, grabbed her mic, and said, "Thank you so very, very much, ladies and gentlemen. You've been a truly wonderful audience."

She turned and gestured toward Jalen. "This evening's been made even more wonderful by having my son hear me perform for the very first—but hopefully not the last—time." The audience started clapping again. Some waved and smiled at Jalen before turning back to his mom.

"I'll be at Andy's in Chicago next week," she said before walking off the stage. "I only hope the audiences there are half as appreciative as you all have been."

Jalen felt like he was falling. He couldn't believe she was leaving again.

47

"YOUR MOM WAS SO SUPER," CAT GUSHED IN THE
Range Rover a few minutes later.

"She's got quite a talent, if I'm any judge," Mrs. H said.

After a short period of awkward silence, Cat exploded. "Why are you acting like Mr. Gloom and Doom? You're sitting there looking like a trainee Marvel supervillain."

"Don't you think it's wonderful how things are lining up for your mother, Jalen? She and George dined with a club owner on Wednesday, he hears that his act for next week is sick and slots your mother right in. She still gets to come to your game. Wonderful, really," Mrs. Hewlett said reassuringly.

"Sure, yeah, it's super for her," Jalen reluctantly

admitted. "But that doesn't make it super for me."

"Why not?" Cat asked.

"Because I thought that . . . after all this time, she finally came home and wanted to be with me and . . ."

"Your dad?" Cat asked.

"I don't know. Yeah, sure, be with my dad, too."

"You can't control what people do, Jalen," Mrs. H said in a serious adult-to-kid tone of voice.

Jalen thought in silence for a minute or so and whispered to nobody in particular, "You can hope."

48

DANIEL HAD FLOWN ONCE, TO DISNEY WORLD
with his mom and dad, but this was Jalen's first time on
an airplane. Their flight was super early, and they got to
the airport before the sun was even out.

Gertzy insisted that Jalen take the window seat. He
clutched the armrests with white knuckles as they raced
down the runway. The plane shot up into the air, and his
stomach dropped as he was forced against the back of the
seat by gravity. They rose up over a lake, then more trees.

Daniel looked over the back of his seat next to Fanny
and dangled something in front of Jalen. "Barf bag."

Jalen ignored Daniel's teasing but gripped tighter still
as the plane dipped its wing and began a long, slow turn

as they climbed. Cars crawled like huge ants on strings of highways. Houses and buildings were like toys. The plane tilted back, revealing the breathtaking sight of land far below them, stretching as far as he could see.

Gertzy removed his headset and pointed to the screen in front of his seat. "They're replaying the Yankees game from last night on channel fifty-one."

"Thanks, I'm good." Jalen turned back to the window.

Gertzy nudged him again. "They trade JY and you're not a fan anymore?"

"No, I am. I'm just looking at everything. It's . . . brilliant."

"Brilliant?" Gertzy looked puzzled.

"Dope. It's like that." Jalen turned back to the window.

When the plane bumped and the window went gray, Jalen jumped and grabbed on tight again. "What's that?"

Gertzy didn't bother to remove his headset, and he kept his focus on the TV. "Just clouds."

"Barf bag?" Daniel turned again and dangled it hopefully.

Jalen pushed the bag back where it came from.

Daniel and Fanny burst out laughing.

"You guys think it's less lame the more you do it?" Gertzy asked testily.

After another quick bump, the plane tore above the

clouds. In the bright sunlight, the sea of puffy white cotton stretched on forever. Jalen relaxed and breathed deeply, staring.

"Brilliant," he said in a voice no one else could hear.

Minutes and miles of puffy clouds later, he turned on his on TV and switched to the game.

A little over two hours later, they arrived. Landing was less than brilliant. There were thunderstorms over Tampa and the plane rocked back and forth.

"I'm glad my mom and dad are taking a later flight," Gertzy said, right after a crash of thunder boomed outside the plane. The window flashed with bright sun and dark clouds as they bounced up and down through the storm. The wing outside wobbled like a Jell-O mold.

Daniel wasn't fooling around anymore, and the look on Gertzy's face told Jalen they were going to crash.

49

THE WHEELS TOUCHED THE GROUND AND THE
plane shuddered and creaked, as if it were coming apart
at the seams. It felt like they were going at rocket speed,
even as the pilot continued slowing the plane, again pushing Jalen back in his seat. With a final thump that strained
his seat belt, they were solidly on the runway, but still
moving way too fast for Jalen. His fingers were digging
into the armrests again, but he wasn't the only one this
time. Gertzy and everyone else Jalen could see also had
white-knuckle grips and faces pale with fear.

The pilot pumped the brakes, testing everyone's neck
strength, and finally the plane rolled to a stop. The cabin
erupted in cheers. Jalen was shaking, but he removed the

paper bag from his seat pocket and dangled it between the seats in front of him. "Barf bag?"

Fanny snatched it away from him and filled it with vomit.

The smell quickly filled their part of the cabin.

Gertzy took out a pack of gum and offered Jalen a stick. "Peppermint helps with the smell."

"How do you know?" Jalen asked.

"I've been on planes with Fanny before. He's strong as an ox, but his stomach is weak as a . . ."

"Kitten?" Jalen said.

Fanny heard his name and turned around, scowling. "What are you guys saying about me?"

"Nothing." Jalen gave Gertzy a look.

"Yeah," said Gertzy. "No Fanny jokes here."

"Yeah? 'Cause I swore I just heard Genius Boy call me a kitten." Fanny glared at Jalen without blinking.

"Not you, Fanny," Jalen said. "I was just saying your stomach—"

"Well, maybe if some dummy didn't dangle a barf bag in front of Fanny, Fanny wouldn't have blown chunks."

While the passengers around them were taking their bags down, Fanny and Jalen were in a standoff.

"Oh, come on, you guys," Daniel said. "Don't make a mountain out of a molehill."

"Yeah?" Suddenly Fanny was all smiles. He carefully folded over the top of the barf bag and sealed it nice and snug before hefting its bulging seams in one hand like a water balloon. "There's another saying you might know: what goes around, comes around."

50

THE TEAM WOVE ITS WAY THROUGH THE AIRPORT, following Coach Allen and Coach Miller. Even at ten thirty in the morning Jalen could feel the heat leaking through the gates, while sunshine squeezed the terminal with all its might.

Fanny entertained everyone within earshot with his plans to attack the menu of the nearest Steak 'n Shake restaurant.

Under his breath, Jalen asked Gertzy, "Steak 'n Shake?"

"Maybe the best cheeseburgers and shakes you'll ever taste," said Gertzy. "You should go with your mom. Maybe we'll all go."

"Where is it?"

Gertzy said, "It's a chain. They're everywhere down here."

"How many times have you been to Florida?" Jalen asked.

"Usually a couple times a year," Gertzy said. "Once to Disney and then usually to a beach on spring break."

"Sweet," Jalen said experiencing pangs of jealousy. He couldn't help wishing the Silver Liner Diner had made his dad rich earlier. But the franchise deal wouldn't have happened without Jalen's partnership with JY. And that couldn't have happened before he became old enough to use his talents. It made him realize that maybe his mom had been right when she said, *Things happen for a reason.*

At baggage claim, the parents who'd flown with the team said their good-byes and went to the car-rental counters. The players hoisted gear bags onto their shoulders and boarded a shuttle that delivered them to the dorms on the Lakeland campus. Fortunately, they were able to move into rooms that had been reserved months earlier by the team that had dropped out of the tournament.

The shuttle driver played tour guide when they reached the campus, driving them first past the baseball complex.

"Holy moly!" Jalen whispered to Gertzy. "They have six fields."

"And behind the fields, they have half-size fields for

infield and batting work. Pretty dope!" Gertzy added.

"On your left is the world-class Legacy Hotel, with luxury rooms and award-winning cuisine—not appropriate for athletes in training." The driver chuckled.

Then he pointed out the football stadium—as if they couldn't see the huge oval structure with seating stands rising on either side.

Next came the academic complex for full-time students, and the Campus Center.

"There you will find health services, a bookstore, a recreation room, lounges, and a wealth of dining options," the driver said, sounding like a prerecorded message.

"Tell us about the food," Fanny suggested.

The driver said it ranged from a French-style bistro to Asian fusion to personalized pizza to a buffet-style cafeteria called the Servery, which offered dozens of choices, all created as performance-based, healthy nutrition for athletes.

"Healthy!" Fanny huffed. "And I had such high hopes for this place."

Finally the shuttle dropped them off at the doorway of an enormous, multistory dorm complex.

"In through that door and they'll set you up," the driver promised as they stepped out into the blinding light of a Central Florida June afternoon.

And the staff did set them up. Minutes later, the team was taking possession of shared rooms throughout the building. Daniel and Fanny were assigned a room right next door to Jalen and Gertzy.

Peeking through the narrowly opened door, Gertzy said, "It sure ain't like home, but it'll do."

"Come on, lemme see," Jalen said while shouldering Gertzy into the room. The room had two bunk beds, but only the top level was set up for sleeping, with a mattress and pillows, and a ladder against the side. The area next to the beds had a writing desk and chair where the lower mattress should have been.

"I really thought Lakeland would put us in something like a hotel suite," Gertzy said.

"You're the one who said we're the lowest seed in the tournament. Maybe the Lakeland team gets the glitzy treatment," Jalen said, thinking, *This is pretty sweet.*

"No, I guess this is where you stay if you go to school at Lakeland Academy. It's a boarding school room."

"At least they have a lot of charging stations. And you can see the baseball complex from this window," Jalen added.

"Baseball and a bed. It doesn't take much to make you happy, eh?"

Before they had finished stowing their clothes and gear, the sour odor of barf wafted into the room.

Hearing a knock, Jalen opened the door to see Fanny, grinning, with the swollen barf bag cradled in his arms. "Don't worry. Now's not the right time."

Daniel leaned out from the next door over. "Howdy, neighbor."

"Aw, c'mon, Fanny. You can't blame me," said Jalen.

"Don't worry," Gertzy said as he bounced on his elevated mattress. "He's all barf and no bite."

"I heard that!" Fanny bellowed.

Jalen pulled the door shut and turned to Gertzy. "What'd you say that for?"

Gertzy waved a hand in dismissal. "Act like you don't care. You just get him excited if he thinks you're thinking about it."

"Is that right?" Jalen stood his bats against the wall under his bed. "He looked pretty excited just now!"

"He's being a jerk is all."

"So I'm not going to be wearing a puke parka?"

"No. He wants a piece of this tournament as bad as we do." Gertzy snorted. "And he knows Coach Allen wasn't joking about stupid pranks. So leave it. Hey, let's get down to lunch. I want to check out the competition."

To kick things off, Lakeland was offering an all-you-can-eat buffet at the Campus Center. All the tournament teams were invited.

"Don't tell me. You can predict their bat speed by the way they eat a hot dog."

"You're the magic man," said Gertzy. "Naw, I just like to get a look at them so I'm not spooked when some jacked-up giant steps out of the dugout."

"What, like Fanny?"

"Ha!" Gertzy barked. "There's guys you're gonna see who make Fanny look like a Little Leaguer."

"Oh, come on." Jalen grabbed his sunglasses and red Bronxville Bandits cap. "Who our age could be more intimidating stepping out of a dugout than Fanny?"

"Guys who do serious lifting. I mean, sick. I've seen kids our age with guns like Luke Voit. Massive!"

"Okay. Ready to find out?"

"You'll see for yourself," Gertzy said.

Jalen opened the door the instant before Daniel had the chance to knock. "You guys ready to eat?" Daniel asked.

"I thought I was supposed be looking for something coming around." Jalen stared at Fanny, in the hall wearing a pair of mirrored Ray-Bans, like Jalen's.

"Nah," said Fanny, pointing to his sunglasses. "Just look at your handsome grille."

"Good." Jalen stepped into the hallway and Gertzy closed the door behind them.

Fanny slipped onto the elevator and stood with his back

to the wall, hands behind him like a soldier at ease. He waited until they stepped on and the doors closed before he said, "It's what goes around."

"What?" asked Gertzy.

Jalen looked over his shoulder.

Fanny stared straight ahead, as if he were disinterested. "My man said he was watching for what 'comes around,' but he doesn't have to."

"Yes, you were kind enough to tell us already," Gertzy said.

"That's not the same as what 'goes around.'" Fanny now added a leering grin to his mirror glasses. "What goes around is another matter entirely."

"Fanny," Jalen asked, "what's behind your back?"

51

FANNY LUNGED, BARKED, AND FLASHED HIS HANDS.

Everyone jumped.

Fanny, whose glasses were now wildly crooked, burst out laughing.

"You know we got a game to play." Gertzy glared.

"Yeah," said Fanny, "that's why you gotta loosen up."

Gertzy clenched his teeth and shook his head. "Do you have any idea what's going on here? I'm serious. Do you know who we're gonna play later?"

"OMG, Lakeland!" Fanny pushed the glasses back up his nose, and his smile melted. "So we're going to play the home team. Big deal. They're probably soft."

"Yeah, they're only the best players picked from all

fifty states and who knows how many foreign countries." Gertzy explained.

The elevator stopped on the ground floor and they all got off. The lobby was a madhouse. Kids their age wearing their team colors clustered in small groups, talking. The room was filled with nervous energy.

"Bottom line." Gertzy poked a finger in Fanny's chest. "We got into this tournament only because someone canceled last minute, and they needed to fill the space. Our team was probably one of the very few who could organize a trip like this overnight."

"So?" Fanny stuck out his chin. "Now we're here, where we belong anyway."

"I love the confidence, Fan," said Gertzy, "but these teams are the best of the best—the top players from all over the country. They are all juggernauts."

"What is that?" Fanny asked. "Some kind of candy bar?"

"It's like a battering ram," said Gertzy.

"A powerful force," Jalen added.

"Oh, so I'm outclassed by a wise guy and a genius." Fanny snorted. "I'll just think of them as a candy bar until I know different. Who knows, maybe someone else knocks them off before we have to face them."

"That's what I'm getting at, you meathead. We're at the bottom of the bracket, you understand?" Gertzy said.

"We're sixteenth in a draw of sixteen teams. We're circling the bowl waiting for the number one team to flush us."

"C'mon, Gertzy," Daniel said. "We've got a great team. We can beat anyone. We gotta believe."

"I do believe we could beat anyone, but we need to know what we're getting into." Gertzy threw up his arms. "As the lowest-ranked team, we play the number one team in our first game, and that's Lakeland."

52

THEY DRIFTED TO THE CAMPUS CENTER FOR FOOD,
with more than a little tension dampening the conversation. Fanny insisted they all go to the Brick Oven Pizzeria, where you could "build your own pie."

"It's free, right, so I think triple meat and double cheese on my pizza. No, four meats and some fish. That's dope," Fanny said, as the counterman shook his head in disbelief.

Gertzy went for a meatball sub with mozzarella, Daniel picked a chicken Parmesan, and Jalen stared at the menu before ordering a Philly cheesesteak.

"I can't see eating Italian food here when my dad makes the best Italian food there is."

As they searched the cavernous Campus Center dining

hall for seats, Daniel said, "Maybe your dad can open a Silver Liner Diner here at Lakeland."

"There's some seats, right there." Gertzy had both hands on his tray, so he angled his head toward an empty table. Nearby was a table with four players in white caps with blue Lakeland flame logos and a lone kid with long blond hair wearing a bright orange cap. Their nearly empty plates said they were just finishing their meal.

"They don't look like anything so special." Gertzy declared.

Fanny's pizza was a sight to behold. "I should have told them to put some of the meat on the plate, like a side dish."

Jalen sat with his back to the Lakeland kids. He understood that Gertzy, as a pitcher, wanted to size guys up, but as a second baseman, he preferred not to try and guess. He'd wait until he saw them in action. That would tell him everything he needed to know.

Jalen turned his attention to his Philly cheesesteak; it was pretty tasty.

Gertzy, Fanny, and Daniel continued to banter about Lakeland. Then Daniel's eyes widened and his mouth dropped open. "No way is that kid twelve. Uh-uh."

Fanny squinted. "Probably a coach."

"Nope," said Gertzy. "No one throws a cupcake at his coach like that guy in the orange cap just did."

Jalen had to spin around to see, and when he did, the

giant in a Lakeland cap was right behind him. The guy bent down and grabbed the thrown cupcake off the tiled floor. He looked right at Jalen and smiled before taking a quick glance around, then tossing the cupcake in the air like an apple.

What happened next was a blur. The boy spun around, catching and throwing the cupcake so fast and so hard that it sent the orange cap flying from the blond boy's head like a startled bird. The table of Lakeland players exploded with laughter.

The giant licked his fingers and sauntered back to his seat.

Daniel was the first to speak. "Oh. Hot. Sauce."

Fanny snorted. "Big difference between a baseball and a cupcake. But I wonder where that kid got a cupcake. It looked so good before he trashed it."

"Some arm, though," Gertzy said, before taking a bite of his sub.

"He's gotta be over six feet." Jalen didn't try to hide the admiration in his voice.

The tall boy sat back down to his last bite of lunch as if nothing had happened. The din of festive chatter and laughter only increased.

"There they go," Daniel said, watching the Lakeland players leave their table as a unit.

Suddenly and without warning, Fanny dropped his pizza, quickly wiped his hands, and jumped out of his seat. He surprised the player in the orange cap by blocking his path.

"Hey," said Fanny, extending a hand. "Justin Fanwell. I'm the catcher for the Bronxville Bandits."

The player stopped in his tracks. He looked at Fanny's hand as if it were covered with slime. "You mean you're not the Tampa Bay farm team? You had us all worried."

"You might think that when you see us play." Fanny's look was dead serious. "But the guy who threw that cupcake and knocked your cap off? He's not twelve, right?"

The blond kid snorted. "You wish he wasn't twelve. That's Biruk Royal. He used to play with my team before Lakeland gave him a scholarship. He deserted us. Go ahead and google him, but don't worry, he won't pitch against you chumps. The Lakeland coaches will save him to pitch against a real team like ours, or for the championship game."

Fanny nodded. "Good. That's what we were hoping they'd think."

"What?" The kid wrinkled his face.

Fanny shrugged. "It'll make it that much sweeter when we flatten them. Keep laughing, but when you google 'the Calamari Kid,' you'll be crying."

"Yeah, right, Fatso." The blond kid pushed past Fanny without another word.

"Calamari Kid. You were warned." Fanny raised his voice so that his words chased after the kid. "And I'm not fat! I'm big-boned!"

Jalen looked through the fingers where he'd buried his face. He watched the kid go and turned to Fanny. "Calamari Kid? Why?"

"You wanted me to let him disrespect us?" Fanny scowled. "I don't think so. We could end up playing those guys."

Gertzy looked up from his phone. He held it out to Jalen. "You guys need to check this out."

"What is it?" Jalen asked.

"I did what he said." Gertzy waved the phone. "I googled Biruk Royal. You want the good news first, or the bad news?"

Jalen looked to see if Gertzy was kidding. When he saw that he wasn't, Jalen pushed the phone back. "Give us the good news."

53

"GOOD NEWS IS THAT HE'S NOT SIX FEET." GERTZY
raised his phone to offer his proof. "He's only five feet
eleven and a half inches."

"That's the good news?" Daniel asked.

"Bad news is that he's so good. A finalist for *SI Kids*
SportsKid of the Year, and the University of Miami already
offered him a scholarship." Gertzy placed his phone in the
middle of the table so anyone could look.

"You can't offer scholarships to kids," Daniel said. "He's
not even in high school yet."

Jalen was already searching Royal on his phone. "Umm
. . . Yeah. You can. Not MLB contracts, but listen: 'It is illegal
for colleges to recruit student athletes until their junior year

except for football, basketball, and baseball.' And 'scholarship offers have been made to athletes as young as nine years old.'"

Daniel said, "Wow. He's got to be something else."

Fanny had taken his seat and had a giant mouthful of pizza, which he spoke through. "Yah bu oo erd um, eez na pithen against us."

They sat silently, first to figure out what Fanny had said, then to think about what it meant.

Gertzy laughed. "Ha-ha. If it's true, we might surprise them, and never have to face Biruk."

"If we surprise them the first time," Jalen said, "we won't surprise them the second."

"Second?" Daniel said.

"It's a double elimination tournament," Jalen said. "If we win, and keep winning, and if they keep winning after a loss to us, we could face them again in the championship. I know that's a lot of ifs. But ifs are possible."

Gertzy wore a big grin. "And I know if you're talking about the possibility of us upsetting the number one team in the country, you, my friend need to share your baseball genius with the whole team. Am I right?"

"Exactly right. The only reason I wanted to keep the whole genius thing down low was because of JY and the Yankees," Jalen said. "Now that that's over, I don't care who knows."

"You should be *SI*'s SportsKid of the Year," Daniel said. "Baseball Genius."

"Yeah, well, I'm not going to wait for the phone to ring about that, but I wouldn't sleep on a scholarship offer." In fact, Jalen's blood raced at the idea.

"That's what playing in these tournaments can do," said Gertzy. "Scouts know the kids in a tournament like this are gonna be the cream of the crop, so a lot of them show up, especially for the championship game."

They finished eating and huddled with the rest of the team in a corner of the lounge for a brief team meeting. The coaches sat on a leather couch and the Bandits circled around.

Coach Allen stood. "All right, guys, I hope none of you overdid it at lunch. Our first game is on field one at five p.m. I saw some of you eyeing that pool, but it's off-limits until we have some downtime. If we have downtime. I want you fresh for this game. So get to your rooms and get off your feet so we can give it everything we've got. Drink plenty of water."

Jalen looked around to see if anyone had questions, but every mouth might have been drawn with a ruler. His arm stiffened as he argued with himself. Gertzy sounded convincing, but he may have been wrong. And in other tournaments Jalen had been in, it was normal for the lowest seed to play the top in round one. But if they were playing Lakeland, you'd think the coach would talk about it. Jalen kept his arm down, determined not to ask a stupid question.

"Okay, that's it then." The coaches stood to go. "Back here at four fifteen, dressed and ready to go. We'll walk to the field and have a half hour to warm up."

In small groups the Bandits headed back to their rooms in the dormitory. Jalen dragged his feet until he was even with Coach Allen. "Uh, Coach, can I talk to you?"

Coach stopped and turned to his assistant. "Miller, I'll meet you at the gift shop in two. What's up, Jalen?"

"Um, Coach, I was just wondering if it's true that we play the Lakeland team tonight."

"I thought you knew baseball better than that." Coach Allen scowled. "In the MLB divisional round, the wild card plays the top seed. In the Road to the Final Four, the sixteenth seed plays number one, number fifteen plays number two, and so on."

"I get it!" Jalen felt like he was falling backward off a ladder. "I just wanted to tell you what we heard during lunch—in case you wanted to make some adjustments."

"Adjustments." Coach Allen stared.

"If they save Biruk Royal for what they might think is a better team—which a kid who probably knows said they're doing—maybe we could surprise them." Jalen met his coach's stare. "Also, I was thinking. I don't have to worry about keeping my . . . thing a secret because of JY's trade to Atlanta. So, I could maybe help the whole team with batting."

Coach Allen's face softened. "Of course I've been thinking about your genius 'thing.' I haven't pushed you on it because I don't know if it can even work at this level. I know it helped in Boston, but you knew that kid's pitching style forward, backward, and sideways. And, the guys you were helping were two of our most advanced players. So I appreciate the offer, but you need to tell me if my concern is real."

Jalen nodded. "You're right. I don't know if it will work at this level, but I'm up for trying if you are."

Coach Allen tapped the bill of Jalen's cap. "Let me think about it and talk it through with Coach Miller. You don't need to know this minute, do you?"

"Do you know when they'll warm up?" Jalen asked. "Seeing some pitches before the game will help me get in the zone."

"From four o'clock to four thirty, but don't plan on anything yet. I'll figure things out and text you." Coach Allen held out a fist. "And Jalen, I like where your head's at."

Jalen bumped his coach's fist and felt much better on his way back to the room.

54

BACK IN THEIR ROOM, GERTZY ALREADY HAD
the TV on and was watching *MLB: The Rundown*—a preview of the night's upcoming games. "They haven't gotten to our game against Lakeland yet," Gertzy joked.

It wasn't long before Fanny and Daniel arrived, all hyped up.

Jalen looked up from his phone and sniffed. "Why do I smell puke?"

Fanny wore a grin made for mischief. Cradled in his arm was the airsickness bag. "Don't worry, my friend, this treat is no longer meant for you."

"For me! Why would that be meant for me?"

"I said it's not, so let's let sleeping dogs lie, no?" Fanny raised an eyebrow.

"Yeah," Jalen grumbled. "All right. So, what's it for?"

"I think I'm a pretty swell guy," said Fanny with a humble sigh as he sat down on the desk chair, blocking the TV. "And I think I'm somewhat flexible with my humor. No one laughs more at himself than Fanny."

He showed his smile all around to prove it. "But even a big-boned, gentle Funny Fanny has his limits, and I don't think it will shock anyone to learn that one of those limits is 'Fatso.' There is nothing, and I mean nothing, funny about 'Fatso.' It's just rude."

"Totally rude," Daniel agreed, rubbing Fanny's wide shoulders like he was a boxer preparing to fight. Not that Fanny needed encouragement. "I'm in your corner, champ."

Fanny cranked his head around, showing appreciation for Daniel's fight theme. "So Fanny has a plan."

"You mean Daniel has a plan," Daniel joked.

"When Fanny approves a plan and Fanny is taking all the risk, it's a Fanny plan." Fanny gave Daniel a dark look until his roommate agreed.

"What's the planny, Fanny?" Gertzy asked.

"I followed Blondy to the Legacy Hotel—"

Gertzy shrugged, confused.

"The kid in the orange cap who punked Fanny," Daniel explained. "You know, his team is from some town in

Arkansas I can't remember the name of, but they call themselves the Dirtbags."

"No way," Gertzy exclaimed.

"Daniel does not lie. I found it on the Internet. They are the Something, Arkansas Dirtbags."

"I can see why they don't have any logo on those orange caps," Jalen said.

Fanny opened his eyes, which he'd shut tight upon being interrupted. "I was not 'punked.' Punked is when someone burns you and you just take it. Is Fanny taking it? No. Fanny is in action.

"I saw Blondy after our team meeting. He's not in the dorm like us. I followed him up to his hotel room, 634. It's at the end of the hall. Fanny needs two lookouts—one in the stairwell, and one by the elevators. Then he needs someone to distract Blondy."

"Distractions," Daniel suggested.

"Distractions, whatever, while Fanny tapes this gift bag above the door handle. Then the next time Blondy comes out . . . Oh! He's Fannied!"

"What if we made a fake call so he actually leaves? I can do that." Daniel raised his hand.

"That's the safest job," Jalen said. "You stay here and can't get caught."

"It's lower risk, sure, but I've got the personality for it.

Who thinks on his feet faster than me?" said Daniel. "I could tell him I'm one of the kid reporters for *Time for Kids* and we've heard about how progressive his team is, and that I'd like to interview him."

"And take his picture?" Gertzy suggested.

"Right! Take his picture in the lobby in ten minutes. How's that? Does Daniel do distraction or what?"

"Oh, no," Jalen said. "You're not gonna start talking about yourself in the third person now too."

"What third person?"

"When you say 'Daniel did this' or 'Daniel wants that,' you're talking in the third person," said Jalen.

"How come I can't?" Daniel looked insulted. "Fanny does it."

"Well, Fanny can make the argument that he's not really 'Fanny,'" Jalen said.

"I never heard anything so absurd." It was Fanny who'd taken offense. "Fanny would never . . . Who cares about grammar anyway? So, the elevator or the stairwell?"

"Hey," Gertzy put in. "How does Blondy swing a stay in the hotel instead of here in the dorms?"

"Not only that," Daniel said. "I found out that everyone on the team except Blondy is staying at the Holiday Inn nearby."

"So how does he swing that?" Gertzy demanded.

"Money. Mega-money. His dad is a fertilizer billionaire."

"Wait a sec," Jalen said. "His whole team, his coaches . . . they stay at a motel miles away and he stays at a sweet hotel?"

"Not a team guy," Gertzy said.

"Actually, Blondy's dad basically owns the team. He bankrolls it, and he built a clubhouse with a weight room, batting cages, and super-slo-mo cameras to video pitchers and hitters," Daniel said.

Fanny, emerging from deep thought with a mighty belch, followed up. "This'll be really sweet. I never got a billionaire before. So what is it, the elevator or the stairwell?"

Jalen figured the stairwell was the most dangerous because there was no reason to be there. Anyone could explain waiting by the elevator. You could just say you got off on the wrong floor.

"I'll take the elevator," Gertzy said offhandedly. "I can't risk missing this tournament. My dad would kill me if I got suspended."

That got Jalen's attention. "Suspended?"

Gertzy nodded. "Coach threatened as much before we left Bronxville."

Fanny laughed. "He won't suspend his boy."

"I'm not his boy," Jalen said.

Fanny stood. "That's a debate we won't finish anytime this year, so let's do this thing."

55

DANIEL STAYED BEHIND, WAITING FOR FANNY
to call.

Fanny, Gertzy, and Jalen went over to the lobby of the
Legacy Hotel. Fanny had the barf bag and a roll of athletic
tape hidden under his shirt. They took three elevators to
the sixth floor, then pressed every button below six, so
there would be several minutes of delay for anyone trying to get to the sixth floor. Gertzy stayed near the elevators while Jalen and Fanny turned the corner and hurried
down the hallway to room 634.

Fanny, cradling the barf bag in the crook of one arm,
dialed Daniel on his phone and covered his mouth. "Go,
go, go."

Fanny put his ear to 634's door, and Jalen eased open the stairwell door. Fanny signaled that the phone was ringing inside the room. Blondy answered. Fanny began taping the bag to the doorframe near the handle, with a little opening, so Jalen entered the stairwell, closed the door, and listened.

He froze for a moment because the thick fire door shut out any noise from the sixth floor, but there was noise. From his pocket. It was a text from Daniel.

He's coming out to meet me.

Jalen's insides turned to jelly at the thought of getting caught and having to face Coach Allen.

He flung open the door and ran.

Halfway down the hall he grabbed Fanny, who shook him off. "Let's go! Let's go!"

Incredibly, Fanny kept working.

"We gotta go, now!" Fanny wouldn't budge until he finished taping, so Jalen took off and rounded the corner for the elevators.

Breathing hard, he stabbed the buttons for up and down.

Gertzy said, "What?"

"Elevator! We need one!"

Fanny swung around the corner and attacked the same buttons as Jalen. "They're coming!"

"Easy. Easy. You'll break it." Gertzy held up his hands to restore calm, then tilted his head. "Shh . . ."

They all froze, hearing a door open and a kid's voice howl, "Gee-ah-ugh!" Quickly the animal noises turned to curses and threats to some unseen attacker. "I'll get you, you low-life crud. I'll kill you."

"C'mon, c'mon," Gertzy muttered urgently.

The elevator dinged.

Blondy raged louder. Closer.

The elevator doors rumbled open.

They dove on board.

"Close, close, close." Fanny attacked the close-door button. When Gertzy tried to get his hands on the buttons, Fanny boxed him out. "Come on!"

Blondy was running toward them, shouting as he came.

"Pick a floor, Fanny! Pick a floor!" Gertzy somehow snaked his arms through Fanny's defenses and hit three.

The doors began to close, but not fast enough.

"Come back here!" Blondy shouted.

Gertzy grabbed Jalen and yanked him over to his and Fanny's side of the elevator. The doors were nearly closed when they heard a shout.

"Stop!"

Blondy thrust a puke-soaked hand into the crack.

The instant the doors closed, the hand disappeared

and its owner howled, even though his hand hadn't been caught.

The elevator began to go down.

Fanny's face was flushed, and he pumped his fist. "Yes! Did you see Fanny's magic fingers?"

They reached the third floor and broke for the stairwell. When they got down to the lobby, Jalen, Fanny, and Gertzy went in different directions, leaving the hotel separately. They met up with Daniel at the main entrance to their dormitory and headed for their rooms.

"We got him good. Did you hear that howling?" Fanny bragged as they were all hustling down the hall.

"I think we did," said Jalen, nerves jangling.

"We better hurry," Daniel urged.

They all high-fived before escaping into their rooms and closing their doors.

Jalen quickly climbed up the ladder and sat on his bed facing Gertzy, both of them breathing hard.

"Well, that wasn't worth it." Gertzy took off his shoes and sat back on his bed with the TV remote and his phone. "How about the new Star Wars movie?"

Jalen shucked his shoes and sat back too. "Good by me."

Only a few minutes went by before they heard a gang moving through the hallway.

Gertzy paused the movie and they sat silently, listening.

The rowdy posse passed quickly by, probably just some players from another floor. But Jalen couldn't help worrying that it was Blondy and a gang he had assembled. For the next hour or so he kept telling himself, *At least four of the tournament teams are in this dorm. It could have been anybody who did it. And Blondy seems like the type who makes a lot of enemies. Yeah, he'll never catch us.*

Gertzy was totally relaxed, but Jalen jumped when his phone buzzed. It was Cat, texting.

Yr mom's great. George 2.

Jalen texted her back. **Game at 5. Dinner at Steak 'n Shake?**

He'd seen one when they pulled off the exit for Lakeland.

Cat called awhile later to say they were all in on Steak 'n Shake. "Your mom sure asked all kinds of questions about baseball. George knows more about the game than she does. But she's proud of you, for sure. She said she's using her positive thinking to send you good luck in the game."

"We'll need all the luck we can get, Cat. I'm glad you'll be in the dugout."

"Why?" Cat asked.

"I need my baseball genius to kick in so I can help the team." Jalen hesitated, then found some words. "You help me get it."

"No worries, Jalen," Cat said. "You can do it." They

talked some more in that comfortable way they had before disconnecting.

During the movie he got two more texts. The first was from his mom.

I don't want to disturb you, but I do want you to know that I love you and I'll be cheering for you!

Jalen felt a warm happiness rush through his body, until the notion of telling his father about her seeped in. He closed the text to keep the worry from boiling over.

The second text was from Coach Allen.

If you're still up for it, Coach Miller and I would love to see if you can get your magic going. He'll meet you in the lobby at 3:45 to go scout.

That message stiffened Jalen's neck muscles.

K Jalen responded.

When the movie ended, Gertzy suggested they try to "catch some z's, a twenty-minute power nap" and shut out the lights. Jalen did his best, but soon Gertzy was snoring, and he could only lie there as the tightness spread like a snakebite, regretting that he'd ever opened his mouth.

56

BIG COACH MILLER RARELY SPOKE OUTSIDE THE
brief instructions he growled at his players. But the
players listened when he did speak, because he knew
batting. Coach Miller and Coach Allen went way back.
They had their own secret language, with expressions
like "dirt pie," "crab bucket," and "califlubber." Coach
Allen would recount adventures he and Mills had with
childhood characters like "Booger," "Gumby," and "Cap-
tain Underwear," and Coach Miller would give a grunt or
a knowing look.

So, when Coach Miller saw Jalen and turned without
a word, heading for the door, Jalen knew to follow. The
late-day sun brought immediate beads of sweat to his

forehead. He wiped it with the back of his hand before hiding his eyes behind sunglasses.

At 3:52 they arrived at field one. The teams from the first game were shaking hands. The Lakeland Ascenders quickly filled the dugout with their gear, then took the field.

From the top of the bleachers near home plate, Jalen sat with his coach, studying the two Lakeland pitchers as they warmed up, one on the mound and the other outside the third base line. Coach Miller took a program from his back pocket and unrolled it. He looked through the program before folding one against the grain and flattening it against his knee.

Coach Miller pointed to the pitchers. "Number three, Jebidiah Hardy. Number eighteen, Hollis Vandertell."

The sight of Biruk Royal on first base diverted Jalen's attention. He couldn't help marveling at the size of the kid and the gunshot sound when the second baseman caught his throw. After a nudge from Coach Miller, he pried his eyes off the superstar and got back to the night's pitchers.

Jalen focused on Hardy because he was on the mound and the presumed starter, while Vandertell continued to warm up outside the third base line. Still, Jalen took in many of Vandertell's pitches in between Hardy's. As he began to get a feel for both players, he realized Vandertell was not only the better pitcher, but better by far. Blondy was right. Lakeland expected to steamroll the Bandits.

It wasn't that Hardy was bad. He wasn't. Hardy could consistently put the ball over the plate, but he had very little heat, and no finish on his pitches, no late movement. His only other pitch was an unimpressive changeup. If Jalen could crack the code with Hardy, it would look like batting practice for the Bandits.

Vandertell, on the other hand, was money. He was tall and lean and had plenty of heat, supported by both a changeup and a sinker.

Jalen's eyes darted from one player to the other in a determined quest to read their pitches, but that didn't happen.

"You okay?" Coach Miller growled, startling Jalen out of his trancelike concentration.

Jalen jumped. "Yeah, fine."

"Not sleepy?"

"No, no." Jalen's hands were clenched and sweating.

Coach Miller grunted and stood.

The rest of the Bandits had arrived and were filling the dugout below. At the bottom of the bleachers, Jalen turned the corner and walked right into his mom, George, Cat, and Mrs. H.

57

"HELLO!" THEY ALL SAID AT ONCE.

For some reason, Jalen felt embarrassed. He knew enough to introduce them all to Coach Miller, who surprised Jalen by shaking everyone's hand and softly greeting each of them with the same four words. "Nice to meet you."

Once finished with that, the coach made excuses and melted away, leaving Jalen with a buzzing brain and a galloping heart.

"Mom, I'm sorry, but I better—"

His mom lightly touched a finger to his lips. "Don't worry about using. We're here for you. That's all."

Jalen didn't think he could love her more than he did

in that moment. He hugged her and said, "Thanks, Mom."

He turned to Cat. "You coming?"

"Yup." She followed him to the dugout.

Coach Allen greeted Cat warmly and handed her a Bandits cap along with the stats book.

"Fits perfect. Thanks, Coach." Cat tugged the cap on backward.

Coach Allen turned to Jalen. "How'd it go?"

Jalen gave the coach his scouting report, which he knew was no more or better than Coach Miller's.

Coach scratched his chin. "Can you read Hardy's pitches?"

"Not yet, but he's not throwing at game velocity," Jalen said defensively.

"Is that the way it works? You can only predict pitches thrown in a game? Or do you need a batter in the box? Or . . . ?"

"I don't know, Coach," Jalen admitted. "I've never thought about how it works. It just works or it doesn't."

Coach scratched his chin again, took off his cap, and looked inside as if expecting he'd find something written there. "Well, let's go after this Hardy kid the old-fashioned way for now. Let's do some damage."

The Bandits warmed up while people trickled into the stands. There was more Lakeland white and blue than

Bronxville red, and other team colors worn by coaches doubling as advance scouts. Jalen suspected every team came to see what the number one team looked like in action.

The Bandits were just easy targets for Lakeland.

After infielder drills, the Bandits shortstop, Damon LaClair, tugged on Jalen's sleeve. "Hey, Jalen, are you up for this? I keep hearing Lakeland is the number one team in the country."

"Yeah," Jalen said. "I keep hearing that too." He heard defeat in his voice and remembered telling Coach he'd help deliver an upset with his baseball genius. Squaring his shoulders and looking Damon straight in the eyes, he said, "They won't know what hit them."

When warm-ups ended, Coach Allen huddled with them in the dugout. He cast his serious look all around. "I know a lot of you have been talking, and yes, it's true. You know how the tournament works. Now stop getting all wound up about it. Getting wound up will beat you faster than Lakeland."

Coach stopped scowling and smiled. "Guys, we have an exceptional team, and we have surprise on our side. They have no idea how good we are. Heck, I don't know if we even know how good we are. And I know they're looking past us. They have a monster pitcher who's playing first base today. We think we're gonna see the bottom of their rotation, a kid who throws only strikes, puts them right down the pike with not much heat. Our baseball genius tells me he's also got a changeup. If Jalen knows the pitch, he'll give you a signal. Jalen?"

Jalen showed the team his signals: four fingers for a fastball, two thumbs-up for the changeup.

Coach wrapped it up by saying, "That is it, gentlemen, so get your hands in here and let's smack the smiles right off their faces.

"C'mon, 'win' on three! One, two, three—"

"WIN!"

58

THE WIND PICKED UP. HOT AIR, NOW LIKE AN
invisible fat river, bullied grit and wrappers as it flowed.
The dark hair poking from beneath the back of Gunner
Petty's cap rose and fell as he approached the box. Jalen
sat between Daniel and Cat, but he focused on nothing but
Hardy, the Lakeland pitcher.

After a long foul ball, Gunner took a look at a pitch low,
out of the zone, but the ump called it a strike, and that
caused Coach Miller to strike his own hand with a fist.

"C'mon, Gunner!" Jalen hollered. "He's coming right
down the middle! You got this!"

The next pitch was a middle-middle fastball, a batting
practice pitch.

Gunner smoked a line drive in the gap between center and left field. He stood on second and shouted, "Hey, Damon, dive right in, the water's fine!"

The Bronxville shortstop went down swinging in three. Damon trudged into the dugout, but Coach patted him on the backside and said, "You'll get him next time. It's early days."

Fanny was up next and looked nervous. He kept patting his own backside and swinging the bat one-handed. When he did step to the plate, he immediately put up a hand and stepped back to tighten the Velcro on his shiny batting gloves again.

"C'mon, son," said the ump, "before breakfast."

Fanny frowned, but stepped in.

Hardy sent one belt-high and inside. Fanny sprang back like he was dodging a knife. "Strike!" bellowed the ump.

Daniel leaned over. "What part of 'a kid who throws only strikes' didn't he get?"

"It's not always that easy." Jalen said.

The next pitch was letter-high and center cut, and it was as if Fanny had heard Daniel. Fanny took his A swing, hoping to send the ball all the way to the Tampa Bay, several miles away. The ball sailed but passed just outside the foul pole. The few Bronxville parents moaned, and Fanny dejectedly picked up his bat.

Jalen had a thought, but only whispered it under his breath. "Changeup."

He waited and watched. The pitch came in at Fanny's knees, straight as an arrow. Fanny hesitated, then swung down on the ball. The ball put a divot in the hard-packed, dry infield dirt and bounced thirty feet in the air. Fanny took off like a barrel on wheels, but the pitcher stepped under the ball and made the throw to first look casual, even though it beat Fanny by only half a step.

Jalen was relieved that he hadn't signaled a changeup to Fanny, because he'd been wrong.

Gunner advanced to third on the play, and Gertzy looked over his shoulder to Jalen. "Got anything for me?"

Jalen wagged his head. "Sorry."

"See you at home plate." Gertzy smiled and tipped his cap before heading to the batter's box.

Jalen envied Gertzy's calm, assured manner. He smiled at the pitcher and all around the infield, took two practice swings, and dug in. The Bronxville dugout cheered, fueling Gertzy's smile even more.

The first pitch was a touch high, and Gertzy let it go. 1–0.

Lakeland fans were surprised when the ump called it a ball, but not Gertzy. The next pitch was a bit low, but close. Again, Gertzy let it pass, and again it was a ball. 2–0.

Now Gertzy hunkered down in his stance even more. The pitcher, behind 2 and 0, had to throw a strike.

Jalen thought it had to be a changeup.

It wasn't. The pitch came in with everything Hardy had, and Gertzy blasted it. The ball sailed high and far, but Jalen feared it wouldn't be far enough.

It would be close.

59

THE CENTER FIELDER HAD HIS BACK TO THE FENCE
and stretched for all he was worth.

The Lakeland players and fans went wild as he turned and showed the ball nestled in the palm of his glove.

Cat looked at Jalen. "So close."

"He was close, but I wasn't close." Jalen stood and pinched his lips together.

"What do you mean?" Cat penciled in Gertzy's fly out.

Jalen wriggled his hand into his glove. "I've guessed two of this kid's pitches wrong, and that's all they were, guesses."

"You're just starting, though," she said.

He shrugged. "He only has two pitches and he's a kid, so I figured I'd get a feel for him."

"You guys can hit this pitcher without any genius," she said.

"We can. But will we? And if we do, can we hold off their bats?"

Coach Miller growled, "Jalen, run to your position."

Get your head into the game, he told himself as he sprinted onto the field. Hit and field first, predict pitches second.

Second base didn't have the same impact on the game as pitcher, but it was in the middle of everything. Jalen snared the toss Gunner threw to him and threw the ball to Jake at third. Jake sent it to Damon at short, who sent it back to Jalen to complete an imaginary triple play.

Jalen zipped it back to first and breathed in the scent of fresh-cut grass and baking dirt, waiting for Gertzy's first pitch. The wind tugged at his cap. He looked at his mom in the stands. Her eyes were fixed on him, while George chatted with Mrs. H. He caught a pop fly, and when he looked back, he was sure his mom's eyes hadn't left him.

He thought about the past few days. Every time he felt it was like a dream come true, like now, worry about telling his dad—and his dad's reaction—swept through him like a wave, making him slightly nauseous.

He shook his head like a dust mop. He had a game to play.

60

GERTZY WAS READY. THE WARM-UP BALLS IN THE
field were rolled toward the dugout, and the first Lakeland
batter approached the plate. Game on. Jalen crouched,
hands on knees, and looked up at his mom. Her eyes were
still on him.

Jalen had just turned back toward the plate when the
batter smashed a line drive toward the 3–4 hole. Jalen
leaped into the air to cut it off. He stretched and dove, getting nothing but a dirt sandwich. He bounced to his feet.
The runner passed him in a blur. Daniel fielded the ball on
the bounce and sent it to Damon, who was covering second. The runner slid under Damon's glove for a double.

Jalen stamped his foot and kicked the dirt.

Coach Allen clapped his hands and shouted, "Great effort, Jalen! Next one! Next time!"

Jalen knew if he'd been paying better attention he would have gotten that one. It wasn't his mom's fault. It was his own. He mentally kicked himself in the pants one more time and zeroed in on the next batter.

Gertzy sat him down with three pitches.

The next batter rapped a grounder to first. Gunner snagged it and beat the batter to first for the second out. The runner now on third tormented Jalen. If he scored, that run would be squarely on Jalen no matter what Coach said.

Jalen groaned as Biruk Royal marched to the plate with a big grin.

Gertzy stiffened. As soon as Biruk stepped in, Gertzy wound up and let his fastball fly. Biruk's swing was effortless. The bat rang and the ball was gone. Lakeland fans and players alike laughed and cheered as the giant kid took a tour of the bases. The score was now Bronxville 0, Lakeland 2.

Gertzy unraveled quickly. Only seven pitches later, the bases were loaded. Jalen was unnerved and could feel the life draining from his team. If they didn't end the inning soon, Jalen feared the contest would be all but over.

Gertzy steadied himself and had a 1–2 count going

when the batter connected. This time, Jalen was ready. The shallow pop fly lofted directly over his head. He back-pedaled in high gear, calling for the ball. Behind him he heard Daniel also calling for it.

Jalen knew it would be close, very close, but he knew he could get it. He knew, as the infielder, that his call should override Daniel's. That was the how the game was played, and he knew that Daniel knew it as well. But he also knew his friend and could imagine the explanation he'd give about how easy the catch was for him and how Jalen should have trusted him. Still, Jalen insisted to himself that in the end Daniel would play right.

"I got it! I got it! I got it!" Jalen hollered, flapping his arms in the air and waving Daniel off. He backpedaled hard.

But Daniel kept coming, shouting as he ran. "I got it! I got it! I got it!"

Right as Jalen jumped, reaching for the ball, snapping it from the air, Daniel crashed into him.

Before he knew what was happening, Jalen was upended and slammed headfirst into the ground.

61

JALEN WAS STUNNED. HIS NECK ACHED, BUT HE
rolled into a sitting position with his glove raised instinctively. He had no idea whether he held the ball or a pocket full of empty. If the ball was there, he wanted to make sure the umpire saw it as well. So he reached up and found that sweet round lump in his glove before hooting and jumping to his feet.

Only then did he notice Daniel sitting in the grass, rubbing his head. "Not cool, dude. That was total hot sauce. I had that thing, and I called you off."

Jalen offered Daniel a hand and pulled him to his feet. "You almost broke my neck."

"Well, you got it. I guess I can't be too mad." Daniel

smiled, and they jogged back to the dugout together for the Bandits' turn at bat.

Everyone bumped knuckles with Jalen, congratulating him on the big-time catch.

"Jalen, you okay?" Coach Allen asked.

"Yeah, fine, Coach."

"That's good. I don't want anyone getting hurt. Now, tell me why you made such a bonehead play," Coach Allen asked both of them.

"I thought I could make the catch," Daniel said quietly.

Coach Allen scowled, but not at Daniel. He was angry with Jalen.

Jalen was thunderstruck. They locked eyes on each other until the coach asked Jalen, "What do you have to say for yourself?"

"I'm the second baseman, Coach. It's always my call on a pop fly behind second base. Those are the rules."

Coach Allen looked at the ground until he let out a long sigh.

"Jalen, you have tremendous talent and desire and just about every attribute to make a very fine ballplayer. One thing you're lacking, though, is obviously good coaching. I won't say anything bad about Coach Gamble because I was never there, but let me tell you, there are rules of priority in fielding."

Jalen couldn't figure out where Coach Allen was going,

but he knew he shouldn't interrupt to defend himself.

"The second baseman always has priority over the first baseman. And you have priority over Daniel, your right fielder, unless he has an easier play on the ball. On a pop-up that a right outfielder can get, his call overrules any infielder—first baseman or second baseman. It's easier to make a clean play running straight toward the ball than it is backpedaling with your head bouncing with every step you take. Do you see that, Jalen?"

Jalen processed for a few agonizing seconds before agreeing.

"When you put it that way . . . I guess I see it."

"So, it's Jalen's ball to catch until I call it for myself?" Daniel asked.

"That's it. But make sure that you *can* catch the ball before you call Jalen off. Understood?"

They both nodded their agreement reluctantly.

"Right now, we're lucky you didn't break each other's necks. And we're going to go over this in detail—for every position—at our next practice."

Lecture over, Coach Allen turned abruptly back to the dugout. "Okay, gentlemen, we're two runs down," he said to the whole team. "Let's get them back . . . and then some."

Putting a hand on Jalen's shoulder, Coach said, "Now remember, just like the speed hitter, you've got the timing.

Go get the big prize. Think big and you can get us right back into this thing."

"You got it, Coach. Grand slam."

Coach Allen frowned. "Did you get dinged out there when you fell? There's no one on base. You can't hit a grand slam."

Jalen did a double take. "But Coach, you said—"

Coach Allen tapped the bill of Jalen's cap and smiled wide. "Kidding. Go get us on the board."

The coach turned his attention to Coach Miller, and the two of them began to talk.

Cat bumped fists with Jalen. "Major league catch. Now launch one outta here!"

Jalen gave her a wink just as Gertzy leaned into his ear and whispered, "You saved my tail feathers with that catch."

"You'll be fine." Jalen pulled on his batting gloves and took a helmet from a hook on the wall. "You've got a feel for them now."

Jalen left the dugout, rolling his neck. He watched Hardy's last warm-up, a four-seam fastball, as he approached the plate. He circled the plate, took a big practice swing, and stepped in.

Hardy's dark brown eyes blazed at Jalen. He gave his catcher a nod, wound up, and let one fly. The pitch was a four-seamer, inside, maybe high. Jalen swung and connected, but too late and too low. He'd fouled it to the right of home. The next pitch was high outside. Jalen let it pass.

The umpire paused before barking, "Ball."

The following pitch hit the same location, high and outside, so Jalen let it by again.

"Strike!" cried the ump.

Jalen's back stiffened, and he choked down a protest as he stepped out of the box.

He stepped back into the box and studied Hardy for signs of a changeup. He saw and felt nothing. The pitcher wound up and delivered his 1–2 pitch. It was right down the middle, and Jalen started his swing with joyful anticipation, only to realize the ball was coming in too slow and dropping. Afraid he'd miss and strike out, he adjusted his swing, dropping his bat head through the zone and barely nicking it to stay alive.

He stepped back again. He needed to calm down and to see the grand slam in his mind. He took a swing, just as he'd swing the speed hitter. It felt like slipping on an old T-shirt, soft and familiar. Determined, he stepped to the plate and bore his eyes into the pitcher. Down came the ball from the mound with everything Hardy had.

Jalen watched it come and took his swing.

62

IT FELT LIKE HIS BIRTHDAY. IT FELT LIKE HIS
first flip into Cat's pool. It felt like smashing a bottle into
a million pieces.

It felt like a home run.

Jalen slowed down as he approached second base, now
certain that the ball was gone. The thin Bronxville crowd
made some noise, and when he rounded second, he saw
his mom. She was on her feet, cheering.

Jalen floated over third and home plate. Daniel passed
him on the way to the plate and bumped fists. Jalen gave
his mom a wink and a smile before entering the dugout
and being swarmed.

Unfortunately, Jalen's home run was the only run the

Bandits scored, and it was the only hit the Bandits could get. Hardy threw a brilliant combination of well-located fastballs with the changeup sprinkled in to upset their timing, completely stupefying the Bronxville batters. Gertzy battled, but the Lakeland offense was a juggernaut. By the top of the fifth inning, thanks to good hitting by Lakeland and sloppy defense by Bronxville, the score was 7–1. The mood in the dugout made Jalen fear that the worst was yet to come.

Gertzy started the fifth with a shot into right field that would have been a base hit against anyone but Lakeland, whose right fielder defied gravity to make the catch.

Jalen was up next, and Coach Allen joined him in the on-deck circle. Coach looked at him with a grim face. "We need something, Jalen. We need it now."

The coach's words only cranked up the pressure inside Jalen's chest.

"Okay, Coach."

Daniel, who was up next, smacked Jalen's rump. "You got this, amigo."

That was when it clicked.

Jalen dropped his bat in the on-deck circle and dragged Daniel with him back to the top step of the dugout. "Hey!"

The defeated faces turned his way and he jabbed a thumb in his chest. "I got this guy. You hear me?"

Jalen looked around at their faces. Some eyes shone with flickering embers of hope. Others looked past him, maybe with their thoughts already on the video games that filled their phones. "Listen. Guys, I know when he's throwing that changeup. That's all he's got, and from now on, you're all gonna know it. Wherever I am, you just watch me. If it's his fastball, I'll put up four fingers. If it's his changeup, I'll show you two thumbs-up."

Jalen didn't have time to study their reaction to his claim. He turned, picked up his bat, and marched toward the plate, confident and eager. Hardy, the pitcher, looked smug.

Jalen took a swing, then a deep breath, and stepped into the box.

The first pitch was in the dirt, 1–0. The second was over Jalen's head, 2–0. He tapped the plate with his bat and took an easy swing. It felt almost like Hardy was going for an intentional walk. Jalen looked steadily into his eyes and saw his displeasure. That's what it was. The Lakeland coaches must have told Hardy to throw nothing but garbage at Jalen. If Jalen wanted to take wild swings at pitches out of the strike zone, he was welcome to. But he wasn't going to see a pitch he could launch.

With a 2–0 count, Jalen felt like he could take a chance. When the pitch came in low outside, he reached and got a piece of it, but it sailed well outside the first base line.

"Take the base if he's giving it away free, Jalen!" shouted Coach Allen, obviously angry.

Jalen couldn't say whether it was the way Hardy pulled back his shoulders or the grim shadow of disgust that passed over his face, but he knew Hardy was going to throw a strike and that it would be a changeup. Jalen bit back a grin and wiggled his spikes into the dirt. He had that monster grand slam home run in the front of his mind.

The pitch left Hardy's hand and came in at just the speed Jalen expected. It had no bite, no drop. It was a real meatball. He stepped into it, and his wrists broke at the perfect moment, allowing his hips and legs to get behind it. The bat barked, and Jalen knew there was no need to hurry.

Still, he was eager to get to the dugout and fire up his team, so he rounded the bases at a fast jog. After Jalen crossed home plate, he paused to encourage Daniel. "You got this guy, amigo. Two thumbs-up for that changeup, and it *is* a meatball."

"It was for you. I gotta see how it is for me," Daniel said.

They bumped fists and Jalen entered the dugout. "Come on, guys! Let's rally!"

They all burst into a cheer, even Coach Miller.

Jalen turned his attention to the Lakeland pitcher. He held up four fingers to Daniel. After a strike and a ball, Daniel got the double thumbs-up from Jalen. Daniel ripped it over third base into the left field corner. He rounded first in a blur and slid safely into second, beating the throw easily. The Bronxville dugout went crazy.

Jalen could see that even the doubters now believed.

63

THE BANDITS WENT ON THE ATTACK.

They alternated singles with outs and turned over the lineup.

Then Gunner tried stretching a double into a triple. He was thrown out at third but still got a rib-eye for driving in a run that made the score 7–4.

The Lakeland team, however, didn't seem to take the comeback seriously, even after a scoreless home side where they left runners on second and third.

In the Bandits dugout, Coach Allen addressed the team. "Guys, we are in this. It's only three runs we need. This game is ours if we want it! Damon, you start another rally."

Coach looked over his shoulder at Hardy on the mound

and looked back with a burning grin. "Remember, eyes on Jalen. I have a hard time believing that they're going with the same pitcher, but that's how arrogant they are. That's how much they disrespect you guys! Now bring it in here for a win on three! One, two, three—"

"WIN!"

On a 2–2 count, Jalen signaled a changeup to Damon. The Bandits' shortstop swung big but hit a dribbler that ended up in the no-man's-land between the catcher and third. He just beat the throw to first.

"That's one!" Coach Allen shouted to his team. "One hit at a time, guys, and we got this! Next man up!"

"You know your Fanny won't let you down, Coach." Fanny peered in from the circle.

"Get 'em, Fanny." Coach Allen bumped fists with Fanny and the big bruiser broke into a smile before turning toward the plate.

Fanny wasted no time in sending a worm burner through the 3–4 hole for a single.

"FANNY!" shouted the team.

The Lakeland right fielder scooped the grounder on the run and made the throw to third on a rope, cutting off Damon and sending him scurrying safely back to second. Jalen stood near Coach Allen, who called to Gertzy.

Gertzy paused outside the circle.

"Okay, Gertzy, your turn," said Coach. "We don't need you to kill it. Just get me a base hit and you're the tying run."

Gertzy glanced at Jalen, and he pretended not to see. Jalen sensed that before he'd joined the team, Coach Allen would have relied on Gertzy for the big hit. Now he had Jalen in the mix.

"Got it, Coach." Gertzy bumped their coach's fist and tramped toward the plate.

Coach Allen peered at the Lakeland dugout. "Oh boy."

Jalen had a bad feeling by the look on his coach's face, but not half as bad as when he turned and saw for himself.

64

THROWING SOME LEATHER-POPPING HEAT INTO
a teammate's glove at the far end of the dugout along the
third base line was Biruk Royal, all five feet eleven and a
half inches of him.

"What's he doing?" Jalen asked, even though he knew.

"Warming up," said Coach.

"But if they're gonna put him in, why wouldn't he pitch
against Gertzy?"

Coach Allen rubbed his jaw. "Because if they can turn
two off Gertzy—and they've got a force out at every
base—then even if you hit your third home run, they'll
still have the lead going into the bottom of our order. They
don't want to use their big gun unless they have to. They

want to get past us without cutting down the times he can pitch."

"So they planned on using Biruk tomorrow and Monday in the championship," Jalen said.

"I'm sure." Coach Allen gave him a pat on the back. "Don't worry. You can hit this kid. You can hit Jacob deGrom or Gerrit Cole if you just stay inside yourself and stay inside the ball. Right?"

"Yeah," said Jalen, knowing that Coach was exaggerating but loving every word.

Jalen focused on the pitcher and signaled fastball to Gertzy. The throw was hot, but high and outside, and Gertzy let it go by. The Lakeland pitcher lost the strike zone. He walked Gertzy with four straight balls and the Lakeland coach approached the mound with Biruk Royal in tow.

Coach Allen reappeared. "Any hope on getting a read?"

Royal's first warm-up pitch cracked like a firecracker.

"Not much."

"Well, if anyone can hit this kid, it's you."

Daniel had been listening. "Yeah, Jalen. You heard Coach."

"Thanks, Coach." Jalen glanced at them both as another firecracker went off in the catcher's glove.

"Remember, strong contact and don't swing for the fences." Coach Allen sounded barely hopeful.

"You got it, Coach." He'd been here before, only last weekend, but not against the likes of Biruk Royal. He took in all he could, watching Biruk's final warm-up, a downright filthy curveball. He'd have no idea what was coming until it left the pitcher's hand.

If Biruk looked huge at the Campus Center when he threw a cupcake at ballistic speed, he looked ginormous atop the mound. Jalen stepped into the box without looking into the stands or back at Daniel or anything. He thought he heard Cat shouting from the dugout about how he could do it. He wondered how he could pick her voice out of the general roar, with both sides cheering.

A blur on the mound and the gunshot sound at his knees ripped him free from his mental swamp.

"Strike!" barked the ump. 0–1.

Jalen stepped back, kicking himself for letting the pitch pass without even a look. He took a deep breath and thought about the hundreds of swings he'd taken while visualizing this very moment.

He looked at Biruk and dug back into the box. The pitcher waved off the catcher's signal, then nodded and went into his windup.

Jalen saw the red dot created by the spin of a curveball.

He swung hard and fast.

65

THE CURVEBALL WASN'T LIKE ANY CURVEBALL

Jalen had ever seen from a batter's viewpoint. It dipped like a hummingbird, not a baseball. He felt lucky just to get a piece of it before it slammed into the backstop. 0–2.

Jalen stepped out again. He felt a tremor race from his head to his toes. His visualization with the speed hitter hadn't included a curveball this filthy.

"Biruk!" The shout came from behind Jalen, but he fought the urge to turn around.

Biruk, however, did look.

"Save it!"

Biruk nodded with a bashful smile at the advice that had to have come from his coach. Jalen knew exactly what it meant. He recalled Coach Allen's speech about Lakeland's arrogance, and it jolted him. He knew young players who could throw curves were supposed to use them sparingly, but for their coach to hint that Jalen didn't deserve Biruk's full arsenal of pitches was a slap in the face.

Anger burned away any doubt Jalen might have had. He stepped up to the plate, suspecting a garbage pitch and getting one. He let it go, setting up a 1–2 count. Another waste pitch came in high and outside. Jalen didn't think Biruk could stomach throwing too many balls. He stayed in the box, expecting a rocket down the middle.

That was just what he got.

He swung fast and easy and his bat cracked. The ball soared over the fence in left-center and kept going.

The noise in his helmet's ear holes was like the sound of a giant seashell.

The Bandits dugout exploded, with jumping, shouts, and cheers.

The Lakeland players couldn't believe it.

"Grand slam." Jalen chuckled to himself as he rounded the bases.

He threw himself into the mob at the entrance to the dugout, deafened by the howling and buffeted by back slaps.

Cat rushed to hug him, shouting, "You did it. You did it!"

"Guys, guys!" Coach Allen hollered. "I love it too, eight to seven, but it's not over till it's over. We just need one more good defensive hold, and they still have an at bat. So let's bring this thing home. Let's get some insurance runs."

Jalen bumped Cat's fist before taking a seat beside her.

She leaned close. "You know, I'll be doing your first MLB contract before we graduate high school."

Jalen laughed. "I know that's not going to happen."

"Why?" She nudged him gently in the ribs with her elbow.

"Because offering an MLB contract to a kid in school is illegal, smarty. Still, he's some pitcher. That I know."

"And that makes you some batter," she said. "Look at that guy."

Biruk Royal wasn't shaken. He was visibly enraged and seemed to have grown even taller. Jalen knew he had to be furious with the Lakeland coach for taking away his curveball.

Jalen felt bad for Daniel, who went down swinging on three blinding fastballs. The next two batters were shown the same treatment. Coach Allen called them in before they took the field.

"Gertzy?" said Coach Allen. "Don't try and be a hero. If your arm isn't one hundred percent, you gotta let me know."

"I got this, Coach." Gertzy sounded strong and confident.

"Bring it in, guys." Coach looked all around. "Now, we got them where we want them, but even though they're coming into the bottom of their order, you guys have to stay laser focused and play your tails off if you want this game. They are not going to give it away. Now, put your hands in here!"

They did their "Win" chant and headed onto the field.

Jalen jogged to his spot and went through the warm-up with mindless precision. Word must have spread that a big upset was in the offing, because the sidelines were now jammed with people. Lakeland's first batter approached the plate in an apparent hurry to get their own rally going. Gertzy wasn't having it. He struck out that first batter on just four pitches.

Bandits' spirits were high until the next batter sent one into short center for a man on first. He was the tying run. The next Lakeland player got a pitch so wild that Fanny jumped nearly out of his shoes to save it from getting by.

"Gertzy?" Coach Allen shouted.

"I'm okay, Coach!"

Jalen was glad Gertzy stayed on the mound. He believed his friend was the best chance they had. Gertzy rewarded them with two brilliant two-seam sinkers and two strikes.

When he went back to his fastball, though, the batter sent one over Damon's head for a single.

The tying run was now on second. The potential winning run was on first. And Lakeland was at the top of their order.

Jalen did the math in his head without thinking. If Lakeland got one more single and made one more out, Biruk Royal could get to bat and win the game with a grand slam of his own. They only needed two runs, but he'd get credit for four steaks on the scorecard. In the Bandits dugout, Coach Allen and Coach Miller were huddled together, obviously discussing a pitching change.

Jalen gritted his teeth. He didn't want to see Gertzy get pulled. When his coaches separated and did nothing, he relaxed. Lakeland's next batter stepped into the box. Gertzy threw some filth with a two-seamer that left the batter in a corkscrew. The entire Bandits team and their fans cheered him on.

Jalen wanted to yell to Gertzy to throw another sinker. In that instant he realized that he knew Gertzy was going to throw a fastball. He'd seen enough of his friend now to know. He also knew that a fastball was the wrong pitch to throw. Gertzy's fastball had lost its pop.

Jalen opened his mouth to speak, but in that instant Gertzy began his windup.

Jalen was too late.

The pitch sailed across home plate, a flying meatball.

The Lakeland player smashed it.

Jalen sprang from his crouch and leaped into the air.

He went down hard, knocking the breath from his lungs. He knew he'd made the second out, but the runners were racing back to their bases. Damon had been either too slow to react or had shaded too close to third. Regardless, in an instant Jalen knew the runner would beat Damon to the base, so the only chance to turn two was a throw to first.

He cranked his body around and made the throw from the ground. The runner slid. Gunner stretched and snagged the ball in a cloud of dirt.

All eyes jumped toward the umpire.

66

FOR A DEFENDER IN BASEBALL, THERE ARE FEW
sights more beautiful than an umpire's profile with his
fist extended out in front of him for that brief instant
before he rips it back with the force it would take to
tear a soda can in half. Jalen bounced to his feet with
the same force, uncertain exactly how he'd gotten there.
He wasn't there long. Daniel jumped on his back before
Gertzy knocked him over. Soon Jalen was at the bottom
of a dog pile.

The Lakeland players and coaches wore the
dumbfounded looks of total shock. As Jalen shook hands
with the opposing team, he thought some were still in
shock, some envious. A few simply avoided any eye contact

at all. He thought he detected respect in the attitude of Lakeland's coaches, but knew you never could be sure with grown-ups.

When Coach Allen gathered them in their dugout, he tried to fight back a gleeful grin but failed. "Guys, this was a big one. Really big. You weren't born yet, but in 2003 the Yankees were a huge favorite over the Marlins in the World Series. They had three times the payroll, but the Marlins won, and that's what this feels like it could be.

"Like the Yankees in game one, these guys thought all they had to do was show up and they'd win. Game two was different, though. The Yankees took the Marlins more seriously, and they won that one."

Coach Allen turned to Coach Miller. "What am I trying to say?"

"They looked past us and got a butt kicking." Coach Miller's voice seemed to boom off the walls. "They won't make that mistake next time. If there is a next time."

"That's right: *if*," Coach Allen said forcefully. "If we flounder in this tournament now, then they'll all say we just got lucky. But if we keep playing like this, and winning, and make it to the championship on Monday, and if these guys don't lose again, then we'll face them again. If that happens—and we win—then a lot of you guys are going to be on the recruiting lists for a boatload of big-time college programs."

Silence hung in the air. Jalen looked all around him and saw that everyone, including the coaches, was pinning their hopes on his game.

67

"GUYS WITH FAMILY DOWN HERE SHOULD VISIT
with them and celebrate!" Coach Allen said. "You're also
welcome to join the rest of us in the Pines Meeting Room
on the second floor of the Legacy Hotel for pizza. We have
a game tomorrow at nine, so Coach Miller and I will visit
the dorm for bed check and lights-out at eleven."

"I don't enjoy long evening walks," Coach Miller said,
"so don't disappoint me. . . . Be there!"

"Great win, guys," Coach Allen said. "Now, bring it in . . ."

They gave their cheer and broke their huddle.

"Oh, guys! Wait up."

They quickly regrouped in a semicircle in front of their
coaches.

"I'm sure this has nothing to do with any of you, but there was an incident in the hotel with some vomit in a bag that burst at a player's door and made a heck of a mess." Coach looked around with a somber face. "Obviously, if whoever was involved is caught, they'll be asked to leave. It better not have been anyone on this team. You've had a big win, and I want you to enjoy it, but just don't do anything stupid."

Jalen's insides instantly froze. He scanned the team, noticing scowls on the faces of his fellow offenders.

Gertzy leaned into his ear and whispered, "Dude, be cool."

Coach let them go, and the team filed out of the dugout to their waiting friends and family. Jalen invited Daniel to join him and Cat with their moms for Steak 'n Shake, but Daniel chose pizza with most of the team instead. He also invited Gertzy, but Gertzy's parents were there too. That suited Jalen just fine, because he was still uncomfortable about his mom, or maybe it was George. Maybe both, he wasn't sure.

The grown-ups were waiting for him and Cat outside the dugout. George rushed to greet Jalen first.

"Brilliant! Just blinding all around! Great batting and superior fielding." George grabbed Jalen's right hand in both of his and pumped it up and down.

Jalen's cheeks heated like the inside of a toaster, and he glanced at Cat, who gave him two thumbs-up.

"Thank you," Jalen said. "Hi, Mom."

She wrapped her arms around him and kissed his cheek. "Honey, you are so good! Congratulations. So exciting. How do you feel?"

She held him at arm's length now and her eyes sparkled with joy. Jalen was at a loss for words.

"I . . . I feel . . . great. Brilliant, I guess." He looked around at them all and they laughed.

At Steak 'n Shake, George insisted that Jalen sit next to his mom in the booth while he took the chair on the end. Jalen had a double cheeseburger with fries and washed it all down with a cookies-and-cream shake.

"Fanny was right about this place," he said, wiping his mouth. When he put his hands in his lap, his mom reached over, gave the closest one a squeeze, and held on to it. It felt like she never intended to let him go.

When Jalen's phone buzzed in his pocket, he knew it had to be either Daniel or Gertzy. He wouldn't have answered, except he was worried about the whole barf bag incident and being asked to leave. He was shocked to see that it wasn't his friends calling, but his dad.

"Mom? Can you let me out? I need to use the bathroom."

Jalen left the table and answered his phone. "Hi. Hello." Once he was out of hearing, he said, "Dad, are you all right?"

"Jalen! How you doing? How was your first game?"

Jalen entered the restroom and saw it was empty. He felt comfortable being loud. "We beat the number one team, Dad! I hit three home runs! One was a grand slam!"

"Is so exciting, Jalen! I can't believe I gotta miss this."

"It's okay, Dad." Jalen looked at himself in the mirror. "You're a big businessman now. Where are you?"

"Atlanta. You never gonna believe the plans for my Silver Liner Diner here. What a location! Very, very nice neighborhood."

Jalen's throat got tight. "I'm proud of you, Dad."

"I'm proud of *you*, Mr. Grand Slam."

Jalen chuckled. "Well, I better go. I'm at dinner with Cat and her mom, and I stepped away from the table to talk."

They said good-bye and hung up. Jalen told himself that he hadn't lied, but the kid in the mirror looked guilty.

68

THE SUN HAD SET A LITTLE WHILE AGO BUT ITS lingering heat still seeped from the white paving stones in the central courtyard of the dormitory buildings. A flurry of insects swarmed in the bright white cones beneath the lights above. Jalen didn't like bugs, but it didn't seem fair that they were so naturally attracted to something that would kill them if they got too close.

George cleared his throat. "Why don't I take Cat and her mom back to our hotel—it's on the beach, you know—and you two can spend a few minutes together before Jalen's bed check? I'll come back and be waiting for you here. Lizzy, are you good with that?"

"Great idea," said Cat's mom.

"Okay with you?" Jalen's mom asked him.

"Sure. Yes."

After Cat and her mom drove off with George, Jalen's mom suggested that just the two of them go to the pool area. When Jalen agreed, his mom put her arm around him and they walked like that until they found two chairs that looked inviting. Palm leaves rustled softly in the shadows. Jalen rested his arms on the chair and his mom covered his hand with her own.

"You're some baseball player, Jalen."

"Yeah, well, I love it."

She gave his arm a pat, then sighed. "I feel bad that I've missed so much of your life."

"That's okay."

"It's really not. Your life is quite exciting."

Jalen turned his hand over and twined their fingers together. "You don't have to apologize all the time, Mom. I don't want you to. Apology accepted. And you have a pretty exciting life yourself."

He squeezed her fingers to let her know he meant it.

"Thank you," she said.

After a pause, Jalen said, "Dad called me at Steak 'n Shake."

"I thought that might have been Fabio." She spoke so softly Jalen could barely hear.

"I can't keep doing this. I feel like I'm being disloyal to him. I keep going back and forth on how we should tell him." Jalen's insides twisted up on him as he peered at her in the dim light.

"You know what I think," she softly said.

"That you and George should just show up and go straight at him." Jalen couldn't help feeling like he wanted to scream.

"Or that you should tell him," she said. "It needs to be one way or the other, doesn't it?"

Jalen nodded without speaking.

After a while, she broke the silence. "Don't you think it's a sign? Me being here and you winning like that? I do."

"Maybe," Jalen said. "You're good luck. That's for sure."

"So," his mom said after another pause, "tell me about this Lakeland team. Why are they so good? And why would you have to play them again to win the tournament when you already beat them?"

Jalen explained what Lakeland was and how they recruited talent from across the country before explaining what a double elimination tournament was.

"That was some kid they had pitching to you at the end," his mom said. "No way did he look twelve."

"Tell me about it. His name is Biruk Royal."

"Sounds like a show name," his mom laughed.

"Show name?"

"Like an actor who picks a name a movie star should have."

Jalen looked at his phone. "Yeah, he's a star, all right. I better get going, Ma."

"Ma," she said. "I like it."

They walked back to the courtyard, where George was waiting. Jalen's mom gave him a good-bye hug and a kiss.

Jalen's thoughts focused on his mom and dad until he walked into his room and saw Gertzy.

"Gertzy?" Jalen stopped in his tracks. "What happened?"

69

GERTZY LAY IN HIS BED PROPPED UP ON A HALF-
dozen pillows. After a day of pitching, his arm and shoulder were wrapped in ice packs.

"Are you okay?"

Gertzy forced a crooked smile. "I threw a lot of pitches today. Maybe one or two too many . . ."

Jalen went into the bathroom and started brushing his teeth, but then he stepped back into the room. "How's the soreness?"

Gertzy sighed. "Don't worry. It's worse than it looks. My mom, she makes a big deal out of everything."

Jalen finished brushing his teeth. "Dude, we need you if we're gonna have a prayer of winning this tournament. But you can't play if it's not okay."

Gertzy held out a hand. "Hey, help me up. These ice bags are starting to melt."

Jalen helped him up and unwound the bandages so that the plastic bags of watery ice dropped to the floor. Where the ice had been, Gertzy's skin was an angry red. Gertzy slowly rotated his arm.

"Better?" Jalen asked.

"It will be."

A knock at the door interrupted them. The knob rattled, and Coach Allen stuck his head inside. "How are you doing, Gertzy?"

"Better, Coach," said Gertzy. "Tomorrow I'll be good to go."

"Good. Great job today, both you guys. We just gotta keep at it. Today was a perfect example of 'next man up.' Remember, the runs that got us back in the game were produced by the bottom of our lineup."

"You got it, Coach," Gertzy said.

"It was a team win," Jalen said as he rushed into the bathroom to finish up and dump the melting ice.

"Gertzy, I assume you'll be okay sitting out tomorrow?" asked their coach. "We need you ready for the championship Monday. Not that anything is going to go wrong, but if it does, we'll have to deal with it. The rules say, and I agree with them, that if you pitch more than three innings, you can't play the following day."

"What a stupid rule."

"Gertzy, there are thousands of kids who have had serious arm injuries, who didn't have to play by these rules. Better safe than sorry."

"I guess," Gertzy said unenthusiastically.

Jalen came out and hopped into bed.

"Okay, guys, good night." Coach Allen flipped off the lights and closed the door.

They lay in silence for a minute before Jalen rolled onto his side. "I don't know about you, but Coach didn't sound all that confident to me."

"He's like that when he's nervous," Gertzy said. "The glass is always half-empty."

"We just beat the number one team," Jalen said.

"Yeah, but . . ."

"But what?" Jalen felt almost offended.

"Well, for starters, we sucker punched them. They didn't think we could beat them until we went ahead in the ninth."

Jalen protested, "They ended the game with their top pitcher."

Gertzy snorted. "And how'd that work out for them?"

Jalen sat up in bed. "I emptied the bases with a moon

shot."

Gertzy chuckled softly. "Then what happened? He woke up and crushed us. And did you see me? I was hanging on by a burning thread. You put any one of our other pitchers, like Hot Sauce, in there, and they're gonna have a picnic."

"Daniel's been getting a lot better! Coach has been giving him extra time."

"Come on. You think we'll see anything but people's ace pitchers from now on?"

After a moment, Jalen lay back down with a heavy sigh. "So what! If we can beat the number one team, we can beat any team."

"We're not even close to bad, but all these teams are great. And we can be great. We just proved it. But do we have the depth to be great with our three and four pitchers? 'Cause sooner or later at one of these shindigs, we're gonna need them to shut down an entire lineup of batters as good as you and me, maybe better. Although the way you're going, there may not be anyone better than you.

"Besides," Gertzy added, "do you really think all these other guys are as focused as you and me?"

As if on cue, Fanny and Daniel exploded into laughter they could hear through the wall. One of them was also pounding on it with his fist.

When the laughter stopped, it wasn't ten seconds before more muffled noise seeped through the wall.

"What are they saying?" Gertzy asked.

Jalen paused to listen, to be sure. "We're number one."

Gertzy said, "I guess that's true. For now."

70

THE NEXT DAY THE BRONXVILLE BANDITS
continued to impress people by beating the eighth-ranked team from Dallas. Jalen had two dingers and grounded out once. Daniel closed the game, giving up three hits, but no runs. After lunch they went to the dormitory pool. Atop Fanny's shoulders, Daniel carried a palm frond while Fanny paraded around, proclaiming him Caesar of Baseball.

Saturday afternoon, in the broiling heat, the Bandits faced the number-five-seeded team: the San Diego Seals. Spirits were so high that Gunner suggested they change their pregame chant to, "We're number one!" Jalen suspected that Fanny had put him up to it. Coach Allen snapped his reply. "You better not think this is going to be easy. It isn't."

The Bandits got smoked 11–1.

Jalen homered, producing the only run they got on a solo dinger. He also had a double and a strikeout. Daniel pitched the first two innings, giving up seven runs before getting yanked. Coach said he hated to say he told them so, and Jalen hated hearing it.

That evening Cat and her mom went to visit friends in Tampa, so it was just Jalen's mom and George with him. They went into Tampa for a meal at a famous steak house that George had heard of called Bern's. Jalen had never seen anything like it. Black-and-white marble floors, statues, and red velvet gilded chairs were everywhere. The food didn't disappoint. They had gigantic chilled shrimp, thick, juicy steaks, and molten chocolate cake with ice cream.

They managed to avoid talking about baseball until the last half of dessert, when they ran out of other conversational topics.

Finally Jalen sighed and said, "Coach said we can still win this tournament."

"Of course you can," Jalen's mom said.

George held up a fist. "To quote Churchill, 'Never give in, never give in, never, never, never'!"

"Yeah, well, we're not giving in, that's for sure. We're in the loser's bracket now," Jalen said. "But if we win in the morning, we'll probably face Lakeland again."

"You beat them once already," said George.

"True."

"That's the spirit." George gave Jalen a satisfied nod.

Back at the dorm, Jalen found Gertzy packed in ice. "Déjà vu all over again."

Gertzy smiled weakly. "Yeah, Coach wants me ready to pitch tomorrow in case we play Lakeland. I think he's convinced that I'm the only pitcher who won't wet my pants going up against those guys."

"Probably true." Jalen pointed at the wall. "All quiet over there with Daniel and Fanny?"

"Like napping babies."

"Sweet." Jalen ducked into the bathroom to brush his teeth.

He was finished and in bed when Coach Allen came by and checked on them "Big day tomorrow, guys. Rest up."

They lay in the dark for several minutes before Jalen said, "Like we needed a reminder that tomorrow is a big day, right?"

It took a while before he realized that Gertzy was already asleep.

71

SUNDAY MORNING THE BANDITS GOT PAST THE
twelfth-ranked team, the Colonels from Louisville, 8–6.
Jalen kept his home-run streak alive by adding another
moon shot to go with a single, a punch-out, and a double
play in the field.

Excited, the team ate together at the Campus Center.
Jalen had chicken and steak quesadillas that were
amazing. His teammates raved about everything from the
cheeseburgers to the double play in the third inning.

After lunch they had a team meeting, where the coaches
confirmed that Lakeland had just won their game. "So
we've got some time. We'll be on field one again at five
o'clock. Gertzy? You gonna be ready to go?"

Gertzy rotated his shoulder. "You bet, Coach. Let's win this!"

"That's great. Really great. Guys, we figured we'd see Lakeland again. We knew we'd probably have to beat them twice to win this thing, and here we are. No big deal. We beat 'em once, we can beat 'em again. Okay, go back to your rooms, get off your feet, and drink plenty of water."

It was a short walk back, but by the time they got into the lobby, where the AC was blasting, Jalen was sweating.

When he saw Blondy, the blond-haired kid in the orange cap, from the Somewhere, Arkansas Dirtbags, pointing at him, with his other hand tugging the arm of a Lakeland employee, he began to sweat even harder. Jalen looked the other way and kept walking, only faster. He passed Gertzy and stepped onto the elevator just as the doors were closing. He saw a look of horror on Fanny's and Daniel's faces before he felt the man's hand clamp onto his shoulder.

The elevator doors reopened and began to buzz.

"We've got you!"

72

BLONDY POINTED AT FANNY AND SAID, "THAT'S the other one, the big kid."

"You need to come with me too," the Lakeland official said, pointing at Fanny.

Fanny's eyes got big and his mouth fell open. He looked at Daniel and Gertzy as if they could help him, but he didn't say a word. The official led Jalen and Fanny to a door behind the Lakeland Academy welcome desk, then took Fanny into an office and Jalen to what looked like an employee break room.

Jalen sat with his face buried in his hands. He cursed himself. He knew better than to go along with Fanny's pranks. He knew the tournament was over for him but wondered if this would cost him his place on the team as well.

If he couldn't play for the Bandits or his old Rockton team, he didn't know who he could play for.

The idea that he might have ruined his whole baseball career, all because of a stupid joke, made his heart freeze. His mom would probably brush it off, but the embarrassment of having to tell his father made his head spin. His father, who believed Jalen could do no wrong, would be utterly shocked. And disappointed.

Time stood still.

Finally he heard voices, the door opened, and in came Coach Allen, wearing a scowl that could melt cheese.

"Jalen, do you know why you're here?" Coach Allen asked.

Jalen could only nod without looking up.

Coach Allen patted his back and sighed. "I hate to play this next game at anything less than full strength, but there's really nothing I can do."

Jalen fought back tears of relief. That didn't sound like Coach was going to bounce him from the team. He looked up because he thought that was the right thing to do. "I—I'm sorry, Coach."

Coach Allen's face softened. "Well, I wish he'd listened to you too, but you can only lead a horse to water. You can't make it drink."

"Uhh . . ."

"Yeah, Fanny told them everything, how you warned him not to do it, how you and Daniel and Gertzy tried to flush the barf bag and keep him in the room." Coach thumped him again on the back. "C'mon. Fanny's out of the tournament. I need to tell Teddy Smart he's playing catcher."

Jalen followed his coach while sorting out what he'd just heard. Fanny was waiting outside the manager's office with his chin on his chest.

"Let's go, knucklehead," said Coach to Fanny as they passed.

73

"YOU'RE SURPRISED?" ASKED GERTZY. "NOT ME.
That's my Fanny, a team player till the end. Besides, the
whole thing was his idea. Hey, watch that thing. You're
gonna break the mirror and then they'll kick *us* out too."

"I can't believe he thought that fast. I almost peed my
pants when that Lakeland guy grabbed me." Jalen swung
his speed hitter again and it popped like a firecracker.

"Are you gonna stop that?"

"I can't just sit here watching TV. I gotta do something, and this can only help." Jalen took another swing.
It popped like all the rest. "Biruk Royal is gonna feed me
that vicious curve, and my bat's gotta be on time if I'm
going to do my part."

Gertzy snorted. "Bruh, you've done a lot more than your share. Are you kidding?"

"Thanks, Gertzy."

"Don't thank me," Gertzy said. "I'm thanking you for putting us on the map. Do you know how many college coaches are gonna see us play? Everyone wants to see the team that brought down the mighty Lakeland Ascenders."

Jalen took a swing. "We're not gonna sneak up on them this time."

"Hey, we don't need to. You do your thing and I do mine and we can beat anyone."

Jalen took another swing, only this time he didn't connect.

74

WHEN JALEN SAW CAT IN THE DUGOUT, SHE BIT
her lip and gave him a nod.

"You read my mind," he said.

"I saw coaches from Georgia, Florida State, Baylor, Miami, and Vanderbilt," Cat said. "And those are just the ones wearing college gear. At a 13U tournament."

Jalen dumped his bag behind her. "Please, I'm already sweating."

Cat squinted at the sky. "I thought those clouds would cool things down."

"As long as we don't get rained out." Jalen headed out on the field. He was all business and didn't even look up in the stands. He felt those coaches' eyes on him and was

GRAND SLAM

determined to show them what he could do.

In that mode, before Jalen knew it, he was finishing up the last few lines of the national anthem and was ready to jump out of his skin.

With Teddy Smart in for Fanny, Coach Allen moved Gertzy and Jalen up in the order. In the first inning, Royal, the towering Laketown pitcher, sat down the first three batters easily. Only Gertzy made contact, with a grounder that was an easy play for the shortstop to throw him out at first.

Gertzy answered the bell on defense, though, giving up one hit—a double by Biruk—one walk, and no runs.

Jalen led off for his team in the second inning. He had tried his very hardest to get a read on the pitcher, hoping that he might pick up where he left off in their first game, but that wasn't happening. Royal was a big, strong mystery.

The first pitch was a fastball, right down the middle. Jalen swung for the fences and got nothing but air. He kept calm, inhaling through his nose and exhaling through his mouth. He studied Biruk, who was enjoying a huge wad of gum.

The next pitch was a filthy curveball that dropped so sharply that Jalen swung and missed again. The Lakeland dugout exploded with hooting and catcalls.

Jalen knew he'd see some garbage now that he was down 0–2, and he wasn't going to go hunting. The next two pitches were low and inside. Jalen didn't bite. With a 2–2 count, he had to be ready for anything.

The pitch came in high, but Jalen saw the red dot of a curveball. He held back an instant and swung. He just nicked it and sent the ball crashing into the backstop. A frown passed over Biruk's face. It was there and gone, but Jalen knew he'd created some doubt in Biruk's mind.

During the pitcher's windup, it came to Jalen. He just knew it was a fastball.

Jalen swung with all his might.

75

WHEN JALEN WHIFFED, THE LAKELAND PLAYERS
went wild. It was their first moment of true payback.
Jalen brushed it off like it was no big deal, even though
it was. Teddy grounded out, and Daniel whiffed as well.
The Bandits gave a collective groan and reached for
their gloves.

Cat leaned close to Jalen's ear. "C'mon, Jalen, get these
guys pumped up. They'll listen to you."

"I know what he's throwing," he whispered in her ear.

Her eyes widened. "Why aren't you telling everyone?"

He frowned at her. "I knew what was coming and I
couldn't hit them. You think it'll help any of these guys
other than Gertzy? I'm worried it'll make things worse."

"It can't get any worse."

"I gotta go." Jalen adjusted his sunglasses and took the field.

He thought about Cat's words while Gertzy went to work on the bottom of Lakeland's order, where there wasn't a big drop-off like there was with the Bandits. When Jalen scooped up a grounder and stepped on second for the third out, Gertzy had given up zero runs.

Jalen gave Cat a look when he got back to the dugout and then told Coach Allen that he had a read on Biruk.

"You do?" A spark of hope glimmered in the coach's eyes. He called his team together, and Jalen reviewed the signs for them.

"He uses mostly a fastball and his curve," Jalen said, "but I've seen a sinker and a changeup, too. If I don't know, I'll shake my head."

As Jalen feared, the bottom of their lineup couldn't hit Biruk even when they knew the pitches. The three of them collapsed like a house of cards. The score was still tied: 0–0.

When Biruk stepped to the plate leading off for Lakeland in the bottom of the third inning, he pointed his bat at the left-field fence. His teammates were tickled and began to chant his name. Gertzy wound up and threw some heat, but Biruk blasted it, and the ball sailed over the left-field fence, right where he said he would put it. As he jogged the bases, Biruk met Jalen's eyes at second and gave him a friendly wink.

Gertzy shrugged it off and stayed strong, giving up only one other hit and no more runs. The score was 0–1.1–0. The Bandits were at the top of their order in the fourth inning. Gunner struck out, but Damon caught hold of a fastball that looked like it had carry until it dropped into the shortstop's mitt.

Gertzy stepped up and saw Jalen signal a curve. Gertzy let it pass and the ump called it a ball. Jalen next signaled a fastball. Gertzy bit back a smile and smacked a line drive in the 5–6 hole for a single.

Jalen knew he was about to see a slew of curveballs. He wasn't going to swing unless it looked like the pitch was going to hit his ribs, and then he only needed to protect the plate. If it went the way Jalen thought it could, he'd wear out Biruk's arm single-handedly.

Six nasty curveballs later, Jalen knew that with a 3–2 count, Biruk's next pitch would be a reluctantly thrown fastball. Jalen took a breath and thought about a grand slam. This wasn't quite that, but a dinger would give them the lead and give the Bandits a real belief that they could win.

In came the pitch.

Jalen tagged it. Suddenly the score was 2–1.

Biruk's posture changed.

He didn't stand quite as tall as he had, and his fastballs lacked the steam they had in the first three innings. Daniel took a walk and Teddy hit a single before Biruk closed out the inning with a K.

Coach Allen called the team together before they took the field. "Okay, guys, now we got the lead! Bottom of the fourth. Hold strong! Okay, win on three . . . One, two, three—"

"WIN!"

They broke their huddle and headed out.

When Gertzy struck out the first batter with three pitches, Jalen could taste the win. He wanted to look up into the stands to see the college scouts, but he knew they were there, and he knew they'd seen him hit the homer to give his team the lead. So he punched his glove and cheered on his pitcher, ready for anything.

His focus paid off. On a 1–2 count, the second Lakeland batter of the inning ripped a line drive toward the 3–4 hole, only it wasn't much of a hole. Jalen exploded from his stance, leaped—not up, but sideways—and came down with the ball in his glove.

The Bandits fans roared, along with the majority of the onlookers, and Jalen realized that almost all the other teams' fans in the tournament must be watching and rooting for the underdogs.

He trembled now, with delight.

But it didn't last.

Maybe the excitement of the two outs made the Bandits relax too much. Whatever it was, the rest of the inning was a disaster with a capital *D*. A nightmare of walked batters, stolen bases, dropped balls, and misguided throws.

It was a fire drill, a yard sale, a hot mess. Coach Allen looked like he was about to pop every vein in his forehead.

By the time Gertzy struck out a batter for the third out, the Bronxville Bandits were trailing 2–5.

76

IT WAS THE TOP OF THE FINAL INNING, AND THE
Bandits were stinging after giving up four runs in the
fourth. The last two batters of the order whiffed for the
second time that evening.

Cat squeezed Jalen's leg. "Jalen, do something."

He looked at her and snorted a short laugh through his
nose. "I'm Thor?"

"No, but you're a baseball genius," she said, "and we're
at the top of our order. He's slowing down, Jalen. You
made him throw a lot of maximum-effort pitches."

Jalen would have resented anyone else challenging
him like this, but he knew Cat was behind him in every
way. "You're right."

Jalen called Gunner back into the dugout before he'd stepped into the batter's box. Coach Allen gave him a nod. "Good. Do it."

"Guys," Jalen said, "We can win this. We can. Biruk's arm is beginning to fade. If he throws a curve, don't swing. It'll most likely be a ball. His fastballs aren't as fast as they were, and we can hit him. Keep your eyes on me between pitches and this game will be ours.

"Gunner? Fastball, curve, sinker, changeup." Jalen made the signs with his hands. "Go get 'em."

They gave Gunner a cheer, and he raced out to the plate and wisely apologized to the umpire for slowing the game down.

With a 2–2 count, Jalen signaled a curve. It was a curve, and the ump thought about it before calling it a ball. The next pitch was a fastball but came in nose high, and Gunner let it go for the walk.

"That's one." Jalen grinned at Cat before looking around.

Damon and Gertzy both hit singles to load the bases.

Jalen chuckled from the circle, dumped the speed hitter for a bat, and gave Coach Allen and Cat a thumbs-up. He marched to the plate, vaguely hearing the cheers. Biruk chomped his gum, looked around at the loaded bases, and smiled.

Jalen gave his rival a nod, accepting the challenge.

The first pitch was a low inside fastball. Jalen let it go. It was a ball. 1–0. The next pitch was a curve that he also passed on, also a ball. 2–0. He was early on the next fastball and pulled it over the Bandits dugout. After a swing and a miss and another ball, the count was 3–2, as Jalen knew it would be.

Biruk stared at Jalen and swallowed his gum. When Jalen realized the pitcher was going with a changeup, he almost felt like he was cheating. It was his dream scenario. The table was set. Full count, bases loaded, and a big fat meatball.

All he had to do was eat.

Biruk made a big show of his windup. His arm whipped through the air like chain lightning. He had gripped it in his palm so his fingers didn't catch on the laces. While everything said fastball, the pitch came in like a big fat slug. If you didn't know it was coming, it played havoc with your timing.

If you did know, it was like hitting an apple on a string.

And Jalen knew.

77

HE SWUNG FOR THE SKY.

For the moon.

For the stars.

When Jalen connected, he grunted at the same time.

"Grand! Slam!"

He dropped the bat. He began a slow lope around the pillows, just a slice more than a jog, to be respectful. He couldn't even see the ball, and he had that seashell noise in his helmet again. His teammates were advancing too. Gertzy was already rounding second.

When Jalen realized the Lakeland first baseman was staring at their center fielder, he looked as well.

His heart beat in double time.

The Lakeland fielder slid a bit to the left, looking straight up, and snapped up Jalen's big fly.

Jalen's legs carried him all the way to second before his brain fully realized what had happened. There was a swarm of players burying Biruk atop the mound, and he, Jalen, had failed.

The disappointment was so deep that Jalen could only go through the motions of shaking hands, although he did manage a forced smile for Biruk. Coach said some nice things to them all about effort and the high quality of talent and how they now had a better idea of how hard they needed to practice.

Jalen didn't think he could feel any worse, until he left the dugout and saw his dad.

78

"DAD?" JALEN'S EYES FLICKED FROM HIS DAD'S
face, over the crowd behind him, and back to those
sparkling blue eyes behind the small round glasses. His
nerves boiled in panic as he searched for his mom. He
clawed through the inside of his brain for an excuse, some
reason or story why or how.

"Jalen!" His dad hugged him and clapped his back.
"You play so good!"

"We lost, Dad," Jalen pointed out.

"Yeah, but you, you play so good!" His father held him
at arm's length with a beaming smile.

Jalen waited for his father to say something more.
When he didn't, Jalen asked, "Why are you here? I mean,

I'm glad, but I thought you were in Chicago."

"I was. Then you mother, she call to say I need to see you play in a big game." His father smiled as if nothing was out of the ordinary. "They pick me up at the airport. We had a lunch, and they tell me everything."

Jalen pinched himself on the forearm. "And . . . and you're okay?"

"I'm happy for you, Jalen." His father kissed Jalen's cheeks. "If you happy, it's making me happy too."

"Even with George?"

"George, he's a little strange, but he's okay." While his father laughed, Jalen detected some unease.

"You know he'll never be my dad," Jalen said, "no matter what he does."

They both laughed, and Jalen's dad hugged him again.

"Hey, Cat," Jalen's dad said, motioning her over. "Daniel! You guys gotta come with us. Cat, you mom, she's with Jalen's mom. They meeting us at the hotel an' we are gonna have dinner in Tampa. Daniel, you, too."

"He knows everything," Jalen whispered to Cat.

"Everything? Even about George?"

Jalen nodded. "Yup."

The three friends and Jalen's dad were halfway to the hotel when Jalen heard his name being called behind them. They all stopped at once.

Jalen wouldn't have recognized the Lakeland coach, except for his cap.

Even so, he was entirely mystified.

"Are you Mr. DeLuca? Jalen's dad?" asked the coach.

"Yes."

"Could I have just a few minutes of your time?"

79

JALEN MOSTLY SAT AND LISTENED. THE COACH
let his dad know that not only would he like Jalen to join
the Laketown team, he should also apply for one of the
three grants the academy offered.

He gazed at the arches, the columns, and the vibrant
colors inside Columbia Restaurant, a place George had
found in the old part of downtown Tampa, called Ybor
City. The discussion was mostly about him. Everyone had
the same opinion. Even Daniel—who Jalen could tell was
upset—said he'd be crazy not to try it out.

"I'm gonna miss you, amigo," Daniel had said, "but if it
was me they asked, we both know I'd be wearing white
and blue."

"I bet I'll be a short plane ride away," Cat said. When Jalen looked quizzical, she grinned. "I'm pretty sure my mom wants to move to Atlanta to be with JY."

To Jalen's complete surprise, his dad immediately said he'd move to Tampa to be nearby. He said he could easily fly around the country to inspect Silver Liners, because the airport serviced the country.

"And we'll be able to fly in often," his mom said.

"We gonna get Greta to come too," his dad added to Jalen's further surprise. "You watch."

"I spoke with James," Cat's mom said. "JY said to tell you that lots of the kids on the Lakeland Academy team end up playing college baseball, and a good many of them get drafted into MLB. Jalen, this is . . . I don't know . . ."

"Smashing." George declared. "Nothing like it in England. A dream come true!"

"Superhot hot sauce!" exclaimed Daniel.

"It's once in a lifetime," Jalen said.

Cat said it best, better than Jalen could've done himself.

"No," she said, "it's all that, but even better . . .

"It's a grand slam."